It's gregarious and dense with life. From the uncertain futures of a high-flying couple that relocates from Washington DC to Lagos, through a nurse trying to get pregnant by a husband who starts snoring while he's still in her mouth and to the title story, narrated by a barber who is surprised and heartbroken at how quickly he becomes a real expert in all styles, Echeruo's collection is a rich, affecting and grand voyage through contemporary Nigerian life in the 21st century.

There's a refreshing absence of the formulaic in his writing, which makes this a collection of exquisitely observed stories written with bracing honesty.

– Brian Chikwava
Author, Harare North

EXPERT IN ALL STYLES

AND OTHER STORIES

I. O. ECHERUO

FARAFINA

Published in Nigeria in 2023 by Kachifo Limited
Under its Farafina imprint
253 Herbert Macaulay Way
Yaba, Lagos, Nigeria
0807 736 4217
info@kachifo.com
www.kachifo.com
www.farafinabooks.com

A catalogue record for this book is available from
the National Library of Nigeria.

ISBN: 978-978-58905-2-5

Layout and cover design by Akeem Ibrahim
Cover illustrations by Emmanuel Sonde

Contents

Contents

To Indira, Diala, Ulari and Ziora

Aishatu's Dinner

There are strangers in my house. Noisily, they move things about in my kitchen as if I am deaf and cannot hear them. I have abandoned my kitchen for Aishatu's dinner. Domestic staff are busy chopping okra into green octagons trailing slime, and dicing beef into sharp cubes for the deep fryer.

Aishatu, my sister-in-law, stands in the middle of my kitchen, supervising everything. She grabs a spatula from a maid frying plantains and wordlessly turns the brown-crisp wedges floating in boiling oil so that the yellow, puffed-up top, like a fat man floating on a rubber tube, has the bottom taken from under him. The maid, without Aishatu saying a word, knows she is being taught a lesson and pays avid, exaggerated attention. With a nod, Aishatu commands her to bring over the white plastic strainer lined with paper towels. The plantains will go in there.

1

Tonight is Aishatu's big dinner. Those that matter in business in Lagos will be there. The Central Bank governor in a white frock and maroon cap will sit at one end of the table. Aishatu at the other. I will be at the dinner, too. But only because I am married to Aishatu's brother.

Danladi wooed me in his sister's house. Now we have a place of our own. But at will, his sister seizes my kitchen and overwhelms me in my own home. Of course, there are reasons. He owes her a lot: she paid for his education, got him his first job, and her kitchen is broken—a freak fire. But no one asked me. No one put a hand on my arm and said, "I hope you don't mind."

It is evening, time for Aishatu's dinner. I have two sons. They run up to me as I leave for Aishatu's house. Idrisu, my older, gentler son, is holding onto my hand, mock-begging me not to go. His brother Ahmed stands in the middle of the hallway and petulantly asks me if I have forgotten I need to put him to bed. My husband blasts the car horn. Even though the car is already down the driveway, I can hear his screaming complaint—"Come noooow, you are going to make us late." The nanny is gathering the boys when I walk out the door. I see the glowing red brake lights of my husband's car. I open the car door and step in.

The traffic is unexpectedly light on Victoria Island. Danladi keeps commenting on this as if it is a miracle. I don't think of traffic. In the evening's hazy dusk, if you keep your eyes off the road, you see the street boys loitering at street corners. They are a dirty, ramshackle team.

Arsenal, Bayern Munich, Utah Jazz—soiled, second-hand jerseys, incongruously united on this street, on these boys. "Poverty United," I muse. Playfully they shove each other while they wait for traffic to slow so they can plead for small notes. Improvised squeegees at hand, threatening the windscreen. "Strengthen your possession by giving Zakat and heal your sick by giving Sadqa and pray to deter any difficulties," I recite quietly.

Aishatu is dressed in white. A flowing dress that hugs her hips before being released in a flurry to the ground. She has preserved her beauty well. Cunningly. Like a shrewd shopkeeper placing the best fruits outside where they can be seen, she has framed those springs of her youth—her pert, full breasts—in the suggestive, deep cut of her white dress.

There is something like the schoolboy in her walk: quick, jaunty steps, bounding with optimism. "Mariam, come, you people are late," she calls out as we walk through her door. Then she looks up. She smiles. "Heeey! Sister-in-law! You look nice!" She puts her arm over my

3

shoulder while bending her neck to look at my dress. She likes the dress but gently mocks the silk scarf with which I have concealed my hair. "Danladi, Danladi!" she shouts. "You won't let this your wife out of *purdah*. And you, Mariam, you are listening to him?"

"Hadja," I plead, smiling. She laughs. And I laugh with her. Even though I know she likes that I dress the way I do and that I am a good wife to her brother. She is the only woman in our family who does not wear a hijab. She has three divorces behind her - three divorces and a son she dotes upon.

This morning, two hours after we woke up, my husband grabbed me by the waist. Aggressively. I know that insincere confidence, the way he is when he has taken one of those little blue pills hidden in the toffee candy can he keeps on his nightstand. He starts off strong and even growls at me. But it does not last long. I can feel him as he withdraws, limp, trailing slime. He retreats to the bathroom with his face in a scowl. He must hate me at moments like this. But I don't care. I deserve more from him. I deserve to be loved.

The walls of Aishatu's huge rooms are decorated with large paintings. There is a giant sculpture of a mother and child in the furthest corner of her foyer. It is made of polished wood. Eighteen of us sit at the dining table in Aishatu's large, formal banquet room. Serving tables line the walls. There are six women. Three of us are married to men at the table. It is the women I understand. Men are a mystery to me. I know things about how a bag is clutched and what is whispered when hands are held to say hello. The contours in a grimace tell me who is loved and neglected. As I sit down to dinner, I wonder what they see, those who look at me.

Nuhu is seated beside Aishatu. Aishatu is still standing, joking, and making seating suggestions. Even though she barely looks at Nuhu, her hand rests casually on his shoulder, like something she owns. I see these things out of the corners of my eyes.

I see it all, even though I am across the table answering a question from a polite Igbo man about to sit beside me. I notice him, too. The suit, the crisp, white shirt, the rich, red-patterned tie. The conscious, self-important air—like the high cardinal of an evangelical church—that only a certain type of Igbo man, uniquely among Nigerian men, adopts when dressed in a business suit.

I see things out of the corners of my eyes. My husband sees only what is placed solidly before him. Nothing moves him to wonder what he is not seeing.

My plate is heaped with fried plantains, moi-moi, and fried rice. Dinner is buffet style with a twist. Aishatu's servants walk to the buffet table on our behalf. We only need to tell them what we want to eat. The polite Igbo man beside me does not even do that. "Just select something. I don't eat goat meat." Eba, pounded yam and okra and *efo-riro*. Giant peppered snails and giant grilled prawns. The selection is wide. I expect the servant to be flustered, but he takes off without hesitation. When the servant returns, the plate he proffers is accepted without comment. I notice the servant's thin moustache. He is confident in his starched white tunic.

Politely, the Igbo man asks me what I do. How I know Aishatu. I tell him I am married to her brother and that I am a housewife. Nothing I say interests him much. I can feel his anxiety. He is conscious of status. He wonders what it means that he has been seated next to me.

Nuhu is making them laugh at his end of the table. His arms are spread out, the left one slung over the chair beside him. He is dressed casually in a blue, simple caftan. Everyone knows who Nuhu is. He is Nigeria's second richest man. His wife is not here. Aishatu leans in when he speaks, as if the words belong to her.

"Aminu, Aminu," Aishatu shouts across the table to the Central Bank governor. "You have to tell the President that people are suffering *o!*" Awkwardly, the Central Bank governor smiles. He is thinking through his response, trying to decide what kind of audience he has.

"You think he does not know?! Is there anyone in Nigeria who does not know?" There are a few nervous laughs. The businessmen are playing it safe.

Nuhu laughs a full, throaty laugh. Eyes turn to him. Aishatu is smiling in anticipation. "You people are all the same," Nuhu says. "You are all thieves. Yes, you, Aminu. Especially you."

The table has become infused with energy. Everyone is ready for hasty words, heated recrimination, and easy conflict. I see past that. I see two men trying to impress one woman. And I am bitter with envy.

Aishatu's house has always seemed to me to be on the verge of chaos. People come in and out. No one's place is defined. Nuhu is married to someone else. Yet every day, without fail, he eats lunch at Aishatu's house. Lunch she often cooks herself. And before lunch, they roll out mats, face the East and pray together. My house has order. People come in knowing who they are. In it is a husband I cannot love.

What is the cause of this bitterness that stalks me? What curse grasps my throat in the mornings so I cannot breathe for seconds, and when I close my eyes, I imagine someone is strangling me with a silk, paisley-patterned scarf? Why do I look around this table, lost, as if I have stumbled onto a strange tribe to which I do not belong? Around the table, no one else questions their right to be here, to eat this food, to drink Aishatu's champagne. To have eight white-clad waiters scrambling, scraping, outdoing each other in creative, craven displays of obsequiousness. They have houses in Victoria Island and Ikoyi and well-appointed flats in Maida Vale. They spend small fortunes on garish watches and custom jewellery, cultivating affected tastes in cigars and champagne. Such expensive carelessness, at the same time banal and grotesque. I ask myself *What am I doing among these people?*, as if the answer is something I do not know.

I am wrapped in this thought, wallowing in its mood, when Nuhu turns his attention to me. Across the table, loud enough for everyone to hear: "Hadja Mariam, you are the only honest person at this table. Tell me..."

Aishatu interjects, "What do you mean by that? Mind yourself, *o*." Aishatu speaks with a smile as if in jest. Nuhu continues. He wants to know what I think of the Central Bank governor's policies. Suddenly, I am a woman gathered with family and friends over a meal. Just like that, it feels like I have been welcomed with a hug into a room.

I married Danladi because I thought I was in love with him. I laugh now when I think of that. How easily we give our lives to things we barely understand. Danladi's promise was always a comfortable life. Instead of a man that wanted a wife, I saw love.

A few months ago, I stepped into Aishatu's living room and saw her washing Nuhu's feet in a basin of warm water. They had not heard me. She was talking to him. He was leaning over, playing with her hair. Their voices were low, so quiet I couldn't hear. I almost cried. Sometimes the words we use mean very little, and the things we think our words define look very different when finally, in life, they confront us.

Aishatu speaks for me. "I beg don't put my sister-in-law in trouble *o*, Nuhu! You and Aminu *wahala* too much." Smoothly, she changes the topic of conversation, each topic—the current Naira exchange rate, the escalating costs of an English public school education, her difficulties with her son's school in England—a footstone leading further away from a dangerous path. Aishatu handles it deftly. Everyone that matters says something, offers an opinion, or, coaxed by Aishatu, supplies an anecdote. You can see their self-importance restored, like birthday balloons connected to a hose and pumped with helium.

Nuhu grows silent. He never takes his eyes off Aishatu. And he is smiling. A thin, grudging smile. I think I understand what he feels. Some distances are just too far to swim. There are limits to what each man can do. Limits to what each of us can accomplish. When we observe another move beyond that limit, covering open water we can never reach, we want to call them back to us, to make them human at our side. Aishatu in the distance is a thing I cannot comprehend. I cannot understand how she is free. I cannot comprehend how she is loved.

Nuhu holds the door as I get into my husband's car. He looks at me indulgently as if I am a wayward niece. He smiles. My husband does not know what to make of it. I can see the uncertainty creeping onto his face. The corners of his mouth twitch, the way it does when men pay attention to me. He bounds out of the car, walks over to Nuhu, and shakes his right hand with both hands. As if Nuhu, in shutting the door, has done him a great service. He is very respectful and conciliatory. As if to apologise for whatever shadow has passed through his mind. Nuhu smiles broadly and claps him on the shoulder. "*Sanu. Nagode.* We should talk more. I understand you are in IT. I hear you own your own company."

In the car, Danladi is smiling broadly. He asks me if the air conditioner is too cool. He offers to make adjustments to the settings. He has wondered when Nuhu would invite him to discuss business. Doing work for Nuhu's companies could be the big break his business needs. He had always thought he could not approach Nuhu without being asked because—and he looks me in

the eye when he says this— "he is so close to my sister."
Now, he has been asked.

The boys are asleep when we get to our four-bedroom
house in Lekki. I look into their room. Ahmed is in the
top bunk, in the bed that belongs to Idrisu, clutching a
Batman duvet to his chest. His brother is on the bottom
bunk. I pull at the blanket that has fallen off Idrisu's body.
The air is cold. I reach for the air-conditioner remote
control. I have long stopped noting the absurdity. It does
not seem strange to me that my sons' bedroom in Nigeria
is cooled, so it's cold enough for them to use the same
blankets and duvets that are used in the dead of winter in
England. It is the way we live.

When I return to our room, my husband is lying on
the bed waiting for me. I like this room. I decorated it
myself, chose the large sleigh bed, and picked the curved
divan on which Danladi has thrown the shirt he wore
to Aishatu's. "You looked very nice tonight." His hand
reaches out to me. I hold his hand. Allow myself to be
drawn to the bed. I give him a quick kiss on the mouth.
His lips part eagerly, wet with saliva and champagne. He
is reaching for my patterned scarf. I smile. Look down at
the bed sheets and then into his face.

"Let me get ready," I say.

He smiles broadly. "I am waiting."

I get up and walk into the bathroom.

I look at myself in the vanity mirror above the sink. I remove my scarf. I like the way I look. I like how Nuhu looked at me when I walked past him from the toilet at Aishatu's. He stopped me. "Hadja Mariam, they won't let you say what is on your mind! Maybe they are right. I see your face. I am afraid of what will come out of your mouth."

I looked directly into his eyes. "I don't think you are afraid at all. You are playing with me." I wanted to say more. At this moment, when his eyes were fixed on mine, when he was for a moment available only to me, I wanted to open my mouth and speak. "I know what I want. Nuhu, do you know what you want?"

My eyes remained fixed on his. In challenge.

He looked at me, and then slowly, his face widened in a big grin. He turned behind me and circled his right arm beneath my breasts. Right in the hallway. Where anyone who walked out of the dining room could see. He leaned back, dragging me into the toilet. Sharply, I turned away from him. Untangled, exhilarated, alarmed. For a moment, his face clouded in panic and anger. Then I said, "Not here!" He smiled.

Slowly I take off my clothes. I wipe off my mascara and then the foundation. I have done this every night since I was sixteen. I do it automatically, without thought. Tonight, I look at what the mirror reveals. Look closely at the skin beneath the foundation, the eyes below the mascara. The heady elation has worn off. What is left is a piece of specific knowledge, hard, like a kernel. I feel like I know something. I also feel like I have ruined something. Something that belonged to me. I know that I will not see Nuhu alone again.

I am thinking of Aishatu when I go back into the bedroom. "I think this was Aishatu's best dinner." My husband agrees. He has turned on the TV mounted across from the bed. Slowly he is flipping through the sports channels. He is a Chelsea fan. He is trying to catch a game he missed.

His Excellency

I sit at the elbow of the curved wall where the windows meet on a curved bench my wife had custom-built for this alcove. She decorated it with plush purple pillows. With my left hand, as if with worry beads, I play with their large tassels. While I wait for Ovunda, I look out through the windows. The leaves are still on the trees, even though the days have started to cool. Soon the yellowing leaves will fall to the sidewalk. This is my favourite time of year here in New York.

I touch my fingers to the window. It is cold.

It amazes me how much time has passed and how many ways I have changed since I first met His Excellency. It is impossible for me to forget that afternoon so many years ago in Government House, Port Harcourt. It was a grey day, the sun hidden by the large clouds that lurk over that city between thunderstorms. Later, the sun would emerge, and the day would seem so different.

I had gambled everything on a rented Peugeot 505. Clean and old, it cost more than I could afford, but a painted taxi had no chance of getting anywhere near Government House. The grey Peugeot made it only to the outer gate.

"*Wetin you come do here*?" a large MoPol snarled at me. His uniform - black shirt and military green khaki trousers-was sharp, clean and new. The Kalashnikov slung over his shoulder, beaten, well-used. It seemed preposterous to say I was there to see His Excellency, so I mentioned the special assistant to the Governor that arranged this visit.

The policemen relaxed. "*Call am for phone*," their leader said. I took out my cheap mobile phone and dialled. The large policeman glowered at me, still sceptical. The Special Assistant did not pick up. The lead policeman was unflustered. "Try again," he said.

I was ushered to a bare, unfinished wooden bench in the guardhouse. I sat there for an hour, calling the Special Assistant's number intermittently

"Where are you?!" he hissed when he finally answered.

"At the guardhouse."

"Which gate?"

"The outer gate."

"What are you doing there? I told you to be here by ten sharp."

"I was here before ten, Sir. I have been calling you."

"I was in a meeting with His Excellency. I couldn't pick up your call. I am sending Protocol."

Soon, the protocol officer arrives. The lead policeman looked pleased, vindicated. His faith in me was not misplaced. "Oya, come!" the protocol officer commanded. His manner was abrupt. He's Protocol. He knew I was nobody. He walked me through two more gates and left me to wait alone in a room that looked like a small, deserted classroom with desks and chairs.

Four hours later, I was escorted through the double doors of a large living room. In the room was a white rug and ornate white chairs, with gold lion cubs as armrests.

His Excellency was standing, a tall man with a barrel chest. He had a large, strong nose with wide nostrils and thick lips that almost seemed a caricature. He was balding. Of course, I had seen him in pictures, his likeness on campaign posters for 'The Action Governor', billboards exhorting us to 'Keep Rivers State Clean!' But, in his presence, I finally understood his nickname: The Bull.

"Your Excellency, this is the boy. Admission to Harvard University, USA and Oxford, UK," announced the Special Assistant. My palms were slick with sweat.

"My friend! Come here! Sit down!" His Excellency's voice was loud, deep, and resonant, and he forced it out into the room as if to propel his power. Startled, I quickly obeyed. It had not occurred to me that he might want to shake hands. But he did. My sweaty palms grasped his. I remember how soft and long his fingers seemed. And how clean he smelled. The Special Assistant stepped into the room. Protocol closed the door. The interview lasted about fifteen minutes.

Ovunda pushes the door and walks out of the bathroom. I didn't replace the bathroom doors when we renovated the large Brooklyn Heights apartment that is now our home. The bathroom doors have been repainted so often that the paint- now more yellow than white- bubbles into thick blisters. Everything else in the apartment is brushed metal and dark wood. Contemporary African art from a gallery in Soho hangs on the walls. Small masks that my wife, Nkemdilim, bought during a sophomore-year trip to Senegal sit on shelves in the living room. The bathroom doors stand out of place.

Ovunda is already dressed for school. At seven, he is the kind of handsome that moves adult women to seek things from him. I often look at him for minutes, searching for proof he is my son. And it is there – the compact eyes, the slight cleft in the chin, the strong, flaring nostrils. But all together, he is so handsome and looks so different that when I take in his entire face, I have no confidence that he is my descendant. Part of it, of course, is how light-skinned he is. Even fairer than his mother.

"What is the capital of Mogadishu?" he asks.

"Mogadishu is the capital of Somalia."

"Oops. I knew that."

"Yet you said it wrong, buster."

"I misspoke, daddy. It's not a fatal fault."

When he speaks, he sounds like me.

I pick up his school bag from the kitchen counter, and we make our way down to the street. Every weekday morning, I walk him to St. Anne's on Pierrepont Street. The good, progressive, private school that Nkemdilim chose. On our walk, he asks me questions, trying to stump me. It's our thing. At first, his mother would come on these walks. Now, she sees him on weekends. All day on Saturday and half of Sunday. It has been two months since Nkemdilim moved out.

"What is an Australopithecus?"

"A kind of prehistoric human."

"It's not human."

"What is it, then?"

"It is a hominid. That's not human."

"No, you are right. It's not."

"Daddy."

"Yes, Ovunda."

He looks up at me, pauses and then lifts his index finger against his lips as if he were a wise old man weighing a decision. If he were not so earnest, it would be comical. "Who is Cliff?"

"Cliff owns the house your mother lives in. He is her landlord."

His eyes go down to the pavement. He is considering my answer in private. We walk on. I drop Ovunda off at school and jump on the subway. It is the quickest way to get to Midtown. On the Green Circles Line, Ovunda says.

Cliff is the Trinidadian man she is living with. She says it's temporary till she finds a place of her own. The affair started while we still lived together. I wish Cliff was a different kind of man- a bass guitarist in a Latin jazz band or maybe a visual artist with an under-heated loft. A second-year bankruptcy law associate at Leboeuf leaves me no place to hide.

His Excellency is in New York. He is looking for a lawyer. Kellerman told me yesterday.

"Busy?" he tapped lightly on my open office door. I looked up. I am in the middle of diligence on a large merger, and I have deadlines. "No, come in." In Kellerman's hand is a white coffee mug with a picture of red, moist lips and a tongue rudely slipping out.

Kellerman sat down on one of the two chairs facing my desk. Our firm has been approached by His Excellency. There is a justice department action. A forfeiture proceeding. Real estate in California, Maryland and Georgia, a significant interest in a bed springs manufacturer in Mississippi.

"Justice thinks he may have stolen three hundred million dollars from Rivers State. There may be criminal charges. Money-laundering. It's a big case. Easily four, five million in fees," Kellerman says and smiles. He heads white-collar defence. He used to be a prosecutor at the Justice Department and knows what he's talking about. "He remembers you," Kellerman added, peering at me over the rim of his coffee mug. "He would like you to visit. He's at the Waldorf."

I grunted. It is not clear that I have agreed to go. Kellerman straightened his legs, placed the mug on a sheaf of papers on my desk and pretended to swipe lint off his pin-striped trousers.

I was able to leave Nigeria because His Excellency made it possible. First to a Master's program at McGill and then a Juris Doctor at Harvard. Now, at thirty-six, I'm an eighth-year Mergers and Acquisitions lawyer at Davis, Polk & Wardwell in New York. I expect to make partner next year. Looking back, it frightens me to think of the alternatives and who else I could have become.

I clearly remember the person I was then. A twenty-one-year-old with a JAMB score of 342 and a first–class political science degree from the University of Port Harcourt. I was dark and skinny, with limbs that seemed to have outgrown me. I remember the long-sleeved shirts I wore - second-hand shirts picked from a heap on the ground in Okirika, checked for fraying at the collar and elbows, for stains and holes, and then the heated haggle on price. Shirts I then laundered and kept pressed which, with the terrible electricity situation and my poverty– was an exhausting feat. I remember the blue-grey handkerchief folded lengthwise and constantly tucked between my neck and shirt collar to soak up sweat. The giant manila envelope with dark sweat stains I took with me everywhere, stuffed with my university degree, my National Youth Service Corps discharge certificate and everything else that could be useful in getting a job. I remember the constant, hopeless fight against sweat, against the stink it left on my body, deposited in layers, day after day. The almost constant anxiety that I would miss the single opportunity that would deliver me from this poor man's life in Nigeria. The absurd certainty that this opportunity would come.

I remember who I was: The offspring of a mother who started out hawking cold, open-eyed fish in a large enamel basin on her head. When I was in my second year in university, she was able to take over a small Ice Fish stall at Creek Road Market, with a small freezer in the corner. Almost everything she made went into paying for my education. Still, it wasn't enough. Every memory, as far back as I can recall, of her sacrifice and love mingled with the smell of fish.

The only things I know about my father are that he died when I was five, that he was a prison clerk and that his sisters irritated my mother.

My first job after university was as a fuel attendant at a distant relative's petrol station in Port Harcourt. I had the second-best grades in my graduating year at UNIPORT. The best grades belonged to the son of a professor with a room in his parents' house, a diesel generator to provide light, a fridge with food, and connections on the faculty. Nothing came from my applications to Shell, Agip and NNPC. Nothing came from the hopeful trips to meet friends of distant relations with *connections* in Lagos or Abuja.

The trips were all the same. Some relative, a townsman, or even a customer, would start talking to my mother in her petty trader's stall. She would tell them of her brilliant son, "with First-Class," who was still looking for work. Immediately she returned from her Ice Fish stall, my mother would give me the carefully folded strip of paper on which someone (she was illiterate) had written the name and number I was to call. (She stank. Even though it's frozen, it is still fish.)

I would call, make plans, and get on a night bus to Abuja or Lagos. My would-be benefactor was inevitably, absurdly, comically, far from any power. One man was a lowly receiving clerk at the Chevron acquisition department. But for the two weeks, he put me up in his small room in Ajah pretending to be helping with my matter – he had spoken to people, and they were working on it- I called him Sir.

I was relieved when the strip of paper led to a job pumping petrol. I had a small salary. There was a uniform. I looked around and started the careful, calculated side hustles that sustained me. The second-hand shirts, carefully selected, laundered and packaged and sold as new in the petrol station's convenience store with the store clerks as my accomplices. The discarded motor oil from serviced vehicles sold to desperate taxi drivers - not as new- they knew what they were getting, but behind the station owner's back. He would think those profits were his as well. The hustles did not come naturally to me. I applied myself. By inclination, I am a scholar. I would prefer to read- history, political theory, the concept of law. But I am also a realist. I had to survive.

Most of all, I remember the rage. The cold, liquid rage that ran through my body, freezing me within. The anger that lived so deep within me, it was easy to hide.

I hated everybody. I hated my mother for her stink, her poverty, and her absurd faith that her church would make things better. I hated Odein, my colleague at the petrol station who would start each morning with a rant, "This place na country?! No light. No water. Graduate dey pump petrol. Thief-thief government. Bloody bastards. One day we will burn this country." But then clowned for the customers so he could get tips. I hated the girls at UNIPORT doing runs, old men chopping them like Cabin biscuits, and then mocking us in class because we didn't have the Nokia phones they had sold their bodies to buy. I hated the drivers who pulled up at the petrol station in luxury cars with their Big Madams in the back seats barking at them as if they were neutered dogs. I hated the *Okada* amputees, the army of former commercial-motorcycle operators, now legless, propelling themselves with arms on homemade skateboards. I hated the entire spineless, deluded, poor masses of Nigeria. I hated them for their ignorance, their complicity. I hated the laughing, the begging, the spitting, the scratching, the crying, the miserable, pointless, be-ing. I hated them when I was squeezed next to them and their baskets of rotting tomatoes in dirty, cramped buses. I hated them when I smelt commingled shit, the forced intimacy of shared toilets in the Face-Me-I-Face-You tenements. I hated them because I was one of them.

The only people I did not hate were the same people that Odein and the runs girls and the rest of our poor miserable mass did not hate: The Big Men. The ones who filled their cheeks until they puffed out and let their guts hang like a stuffed bag over their pants. We did not hate them because they were the gifted ones who took while we looked. The ones who dropped large tips, bought us Nokia phones and paid for our tickets to North America.

There are things poverty teaches you. Lessons that stick to you, even though you pretend to forget. My mother died when I was at McGill. A cousin called, quickly delivering the news before the line went dead. I couldn't afford to go back to Nigeria for her funeral. The woman who had dedicated much of her life to nurturing mine was put in the ground. I was not there.

Nkemdilim was always trying to get me to talk about my mother. She would start about it at odd moments, over brunch on a Sunday afternoon, in the queue at the Pavilion Theatre when we went to see the I, Robot movie. "Obviously, she meant a lot to you. Why don't you ever speak of her?" I did not understand what she wanted. What she wanted me to say. I just stared. "Dude, I love you, but you are repressed," she said, laughed, and kissed me. Those were the good times.

I loved Nkemdilim before I met her. Later on, I would joke that we met online. The truth? I saw her name on the Paul Weiss website when looking up the bio of opposing counsel on a pharma merger. I clicked on the bio. The profile picture with the curly hair, the smile, the Yale law degree, and the strong Igbo name – Nkemdilim Okorie. I came into the office and logged on to that page for four days in a row, leaving the tab open on my browser, periodically refreshing the page to see if anything had changed. Deep bonds have been built on less.

I reached out to a former classmate at Paul Weiss. He introduced us on a conference call as if it was his idea. In my dislocated, confused loneliness, before the chasm that opened up between what I had known and what I was on the path to becoming, I saw a bridge, and I took it. Who could blame me?

Before Nkemdilim, there were the Puerto Rican secretaries and receptionists, the Dominicanas at the Copa that I sometimes succeeded in getting into bed; the

African American lawyers I took to dinner at the Four Seasons, my devastating opening gambit. With stunning regularity, if we had sex on that first date, we would have a warped, disjointed six-week romance, give or take a week. Then it would end. Usually, on speaking terms - they just wanted out. When there was no sex on that first night, there would be no sex, ever. And we would hover around each other for a week or two, confused and frustrated, until bitterness set in. In the end, contact would be cut abruptly.

I never went near the Nigerian women. The ones who worked as nurses at Memorial Sloan-Kettering or as teacher assistants at the Board of Education. The ones that came up to you at the house parties in Queens that you were dragged to on a slow Saturday night and tried to offer you the fried rice and fried plantains they had made themselves while asking you in Igbo where you worked.

Nkemdilim was entirely different to me. I thought of her as an untainted Nigerian. I thought of her as a fresh start for our descendants and me. Even though she was born in America and had never lived in Nigeria, she insisted that everyone call her by her full name- Nkemdilim- no contractions, no nicknames.

On a cold, windy January morning four months after we met, I got into a taxi cab near my apartment on Thirty-sixth and Lexington and headed to Nkemdilim's apartment in Fort Greene. I called her when the taxi got on the Brooklyn Bridge, and by the time we got to her door she was skipping down the stairs. She threw a small duffel bag onto the back seat and, ignoring the cab driver, started kissing me on the mouth, her arms around my neck. Because when I got in I said: One stop and then LaGuardia, the cab driver slowly pulled away from the curb and headed for the airport without another word.

We had to wait in line at Detroit Metropolitan for the Hertz rental. When we pulled up to the driveway of their five-bedroom colonial in Ann Arbor, her parents were standing on the porch waiting for us. Her mother, a tall, slender, white woman, was wearing dark blue dress pants and a cream, thick-knit cardigan sweater. Her father, a portly man with a full beard, had put on the traditional Igbo *Isi Agu* ceremonial robe to welcome us.

"Welcome," Nkemdilim's mother called, heading to the car. "*Nno, Nno,*" her father said, waiting proudly on the porch. Nkemdilim had told me their story. Her father, now an engineering professor at the University of Michigan, had come there for graduate work just before the start of the Nigerian civil war. Before the war ended, he was engaged to the daughter of a prominent Dearborn auto executive.

I surprised Nkemdilim two days later when I asked her to marry me in her parents' den. She still seemed shocked when she joined me on my knees and whispered "Yes" in my ear. I was putting the ring on her finger when her mother walked in from the kitchen and let out a whoop of joy. Her father, summoned from the kitchen, shook my hand. *Dinmkpa,* he said, over and over, patting my shoulder. He took me up to his study and offered me a pipe.

If you ask Nkemdilim what ruined our marriage, she will tell you I was not present. "You weren't there. You gave me no warmth. You don't love me. Ovunda…. Ovunda is the only person you love. Maybe you love the idea of me…that's it. You know, sometimes I would watch you with him and get jealous. Isn't that pathetic? And feeling that, year after year, it hurts. It really hurts. It hollows out your insides." Because what she had just said was true, I didn't look her in the eye when I denied it.

I played it safe the first time I called Nkemdilim to invite her on a date. A Minority Corporate Counsel Association event where there would be people we both knew and easy things to talk about. She asked me if there would be food. I told her the e-vite said there would be hors d'oeuvres. Except I pronounced it *'horse devours'*. It is not the sort of thing I would remember. It is the sort of thing I systematically make myself forget. But during one of our fights, when, filled with anger and bitterness, we were both, in our own way, attempting to understand how we had each brought ourselves to this place, she had reminded me. "*Horse devours*," she spat. "I can't believe I married a man that would say that." The sad thing? I understood what she meant.

In my office on the twenty-eighth floor, I look through a window at the traffic crawling like a line of toy cars down Lexington Avenue. Yes, it amazes me how much has changed. It is not a corner office, but there is a large window, and that means something, for I am not yet a partner.

On the bookshelf at the far wall are carefully arranged bound leather volumes, each representing a significant merger transaction that I've closed on behalf of our firm. The leather-bound transaction binders are a personal flourish, one I introduced very early in my career. I think of myself as a careful, thoughtful counsel, guiding the billion-dollar corporations we represent through the intricacies and pitfalls of what is, in the end, a union as precarious as any arranged marriage. These leather volumes are the physical testament to the care, attention, and, I would like to believe, insight I have brought to this task.

I get up from my chair and put on my suit jacket. It is just past noon. I ride down the elevator and walk out of the office. It is a late October day, the time of year I like New York's streets the best, but I resent taking this walk. I walk down Park Avenue to the Waldorf.

When I knock on his suite door, His Excellency opens it himself. He is dressed casually. Jeans, a polo shirt, and a large, diamond-encrusted Hublot watch. Technically, he isn't His Excellency anymore. Now, he is the ex-governor of a Nigerian state facing potential prosecution.

But the two other men in the room still call him that. "Excellency, make we go, I beg," the younger one in gym clothes says, starting to get up.

"My friend, sit down!" His Excellency booms. His voice has a slight stammer when angry as if it too is trembling. "Here is the kind of people you should be meeting and you want to start going. Where are you going?" The younger man is one of His Excellency's political operatives, the coordinator of the Youth Wing. I guess he is about thirty-five. He maintains His Excellency's website from a storefront in Camden, New Jersey.

His Excellency is balder now, greyer at the temples, but otherwise, he looks the same. Perhaps even, he looks better rested.

"This guy you are seeing is not senior to you. Yet he is a lawyer in one of the most prominent law firms in this country. Have you heard of Davis Polk? How can you live in this America and say you haven't heard of Davis Polk? No law firm is more respected in America than Davis Polk. When they tell you to study, you people will not listen. Look at him! He used to work in a petrol station in Port Harcourt!" The Youth Wing leader contrives a look to suggest that he is remorseful for daring to leave and that he is very impressed by my achievement. I know this buffoonery too well – His Excellency's and Youth Wing's. I keep my eyes on His Excellency.

It is a large suite with an airy living room decorated in a rich, gilded-age style. The carpet is blue with gold specks and gold borders. The windows look out on Park Avenue. Gold-coloured curtains drape to the floor. Large, overstuffed armchairs are gathered around a cream-coloured coffee table in the centre of the room. Near the far wall, on a tray on the floor, an empty champagne bottle sits in an ice bucket. Beside it, two dirty flutes, one of them smeared with lipstick.

"Please, I beg, sit down," His Excellency turns to me. "Don't mind these people."

"Won't you ask him what he will drink," he shrieks at the older man in a brown short-sleeved suit. When the man gets up to ask, I am surprised to recognise Protocol. I don't want anything to drink, but I ask for water.

Protocol returns from the adjoining room with a

small water bottle and a tall glass. There is no recognition on his face. "Can I open, sir?" he asks. I thank him. I will do it myself.

"My friend, how are you? How is the family? You are married now, eh?" His Excellency asks me, settling down in the upholstered writing-table chair he drags to the coffee table. His cologne dominates the air. "I hope you married from our place? That's the problem we have nowadays. When you boys come here, you go and marry one white girl. That's how you forget home."

I tell His Excellency that my wife is from Nigeria. I don't know why I say this. It's really not true, and I don't need his approval.

"*Ehe*, you see it. An intelligent man!" He juts his chin out at Youth Wing. "This one married a white woman."

"Excellency!" Youth Wing exclaims and laughs deeply, as if it's the funniest thing he has ever heard. Protocol laughs too.

"But I don't need to tell you these things. You are an intelligent boy. You already know. Although there is one place that you failed exam." He leans back in his chair and looks in Protocol's direction.

"Should I tell him the place he failed exam?" He does not wait for a response. "As our young people, we, the elders, should always advise you," he continues, "When you heard I had come to New York, you should

34

have come immediately. It's not something that someone needs to tell you. I know you people are busy, but these things are important." Youth Wing and Protocol are nodding their heads in agreement.

I know what they mean. I know what is expected of me. In the world we occupied, survival subsumed everything. Even though he is in the middle of Manhattan, Protocol cannot imagine living in a world where he can even begin to flourish without His Excellency.

"Anyway, let's leave that one," His Excellency says. "After, we will discuss when I will come to your house and eat your wife's *egusi* soup. It's not because I am in New York that everyday hamburger, hamburger." He chuckles and then looks around. Youth Wing and Protocol are giggling wildly.

There is something about their laughter that I find deeply unsettling. They cannot know my wife has left me, yet somehow I imagine this knowledge spices their mirth.

While he is talking, His Excellency has pulled his chair close to where I am sitting so, keeping his voice low, we can have some privacy. The buffoonery is over.

"I spoke to that guy Bob Kellerman. I will give you people the work. I told them they should count you as the person that brought the money. They say they are making you partner next year. What I want you to do is watch what is happening so you can tell me. I know you are in another department, but I want your eyes on this matter."

I draw in a sharp breath and marvel at the ease with which he assumes I am his accomplice, his inside man. I stay silent, wallowing in the intimacy of His Excellency's cologne, the perfume of conspiratorial camaraderie. Our worlds have not shifted.

Youth Wing and Protocol are leaning in. He misunderstands my silence and orders the two men to leave us and enter the adjoining room.

Then he tells me his problems are political. The new president of Nigeria is a political enemy, "and that man had many friends in this America."

"How could you have stolen that much money? What did you think would happen?" I ask him. My eyes look directly at his.

He stops. He looks at my face for a long moment, then smiles broadly. He puts a hand on my knee and leans in conspiratorially. "My brother, did we know they would start all this money-laundering *wahala*? This money has been here for over seven years."

And briefly, the need that took me to Government House, the survival instinct that got me out of Nigeria on a flight paid for by this man, seeks to assert itself, pushing me to answer to his need. To be his ally, now, when I can return a favour. Be a brother of sorts. But I have known suffering, and even back then, in my twenties, in Nigeria, unlike many around me, I was not a sentimental fool. I reassert myself. Coldly, maliciously, in my conference call voice, with my eyes fixed on him, I ask: "You stole half a billion dollars from our home state? You expect nothing will happen to you?"

He leans back in his chair and stares at me, appraising me for the first time. He starts tapping his left foot on the floor, beating out a quick carpet-muffled rhythm. Then he springs from the chair and yells, "N-N-Nothing! Nothing will happen! Do you hear me? Nothing will happen! Look at this idiot! Are you mad?! Who do you think you are talking to?! If I didn't sponsor you, you would be a nobody!"

The loud shouts have brought Youth Wing and Protocol back into the room. His Excellency is still raging, "Look, my friend, I will deal with you! Do you think because you are in America? If anything happens bad in this case….you will know who you are dealing with!"

Youth Wing goes to His Excellency's side. "Oga, cool down, please. Excellency, please, cool down." There is something too familiar, casual, in Youth Wing's manner, as if he also thinks this is a farce in which, regrettably, he has a role. I am still sitting. Inside me, something is rising. If I think of my son, I am afraid I will cry.

I get up, grab the bottle of Fiji water and head for the door. His Excellency is still shouting when the door closes behind me. I walk towards Grand Central station. I will not be going back to the office today. Today, I will pick my son up from school. I will take him to play in Prospect Park.

As I cross Forty-sixth Street, I feel myself getting cold. I start to shiver. I should have brought an overcoat.

Communicable Disease

Late in the afternoon of one of the coldest days in October, my wife left our single-family house in Silver Springs, a suburb of Washington D.C. She was on her way to Baltimore-Washington International to catch a plane that would carry her (or so it seemed to me at the time) on a hasty, ill-considered commitment to a different life in Lagos, Nigeria.

It was planned - and the plan was principally my wife's - that I was to follow in two months when our sons were out of school, and she had completed arrangements at the primary school they would be attending in Lagos.

I pulled her two black clamshell suitcases downstairs, over the light-brown carpeted staircase, through the purple front door, dragging them along the frozen concrete of the thin sidewalk, flanked on either side by icy blades of green grass.

Lifting the suitcases into the cavernous trunk of the

Ford Crown Victoria, I was struck by how light they were and, oddly, by the aggressive cleanliness of the dark-grey industrial carpet that lined the taxi's trunk.

I had planned to give my wife a long kiss at parting. I meant it as a gesture, a promise on my part of openness, willing to part as one who had laid aside, at least temporarily, his misgivings and the arguments and bile spawned by the life change she was imposing on us, her family.

But after I slammed close the Crown Vic's trunk, I found that my wife had already settled herself in the back seat, and the taxi's door was shut against her.

I slowed down and then stopped, standing on the empty street, when I saw she was blowing me a kiss through the large car's back window. As the cab pulled away from the curb, I reciprocated the gesture, my warm breath appearing before me like cigarette smoke in the cold air. When the cab reached the traffic light at the end of the street, I knew it would be another left on Geneva Avenue and then the on-ramp to Interstate 95 and, from there, a direct route to BWI.

As I stood on that lonely street, watching the Crown Vic's back lights' red glow in the distance, I was weighed down by a consciousness of wasted effort. A lot of energy had been expended so that I could be there when my wife left our home. There were patient appointments cancelled or rescheduled, a rushed laparoscopy in the office, and last-minute arrangements for coverage of a radical hysterectomy I was scheduled to perform at Holy Cross. Principally, the effort was that of Becky Wehestrom, my unsentimental, competent practice manager.

I had an hour–till 5.30 p.m.– before I would return to my usual routine. As on every other weekday, at that time, I would leave work to get our boys at the after-school daycare, driving them through traffic past the Piney Branch Shopping Center, where, on those evenings when the idea of rewarming chicken fajitas or grilling sea bass overwhelmed me (or on those days when my younger son insisted that the boys were entitled to a treat), I would stop, pulling up to the drive-through window at Boston Market or Pizza Hut for a take-out meal.

As the boys came crashing through the purple door, one around the other and made their way to the bar stools around the kitchen island where we had all our meals, the rules were simple.

The first rule: Homework first. So while I warmed Special Fried Rice and sizzled up burgers from frozen patties, they worked on long division and social studies. (On take-out evenings, homework was approached with slurps of Mountain Dew and pepperoni slices.)

The second, a rule against which they were in

constant rebellion, required a bath every night. None of their friends, I would constantly be reminded, had to take a bath at night. It was a position from which I could not be moved, the holdover of a childhood in Nigeria, where the relentless heat and humidity of the day had elevated the evening bath into a fundamental act of hygiene and civilisation.

So I carry Ebitu, my six-year-old boy, into the large bathtub, pour water gathered in a repurposed Tupperware plastic container over his head, lather his hair and body with Irish Spring bath gel and then scrub him with a square wash towel.

Ebitu's eight-year-old brother prefers to take a shower. He walks into the bathroom with a towel tied around his waist, looks over to his brother, covered head to foot in soap suds, and says: "You look like an alien." And sweet Ebitu smiles and tries to open his eyes to see, pops close one eye and zaps his brother with an imaginary laser gun. Ebitu and I laugh loudly at his brother's death dance.

The boys are accustomed to their mother's absences - to attend medical conferences, do field studies, and lobby bureaucrats in Delhi, Dar Es Salam and Bangkok. The travel is a requirement of her international health career.

It was not until I was drying Ebitu's hair that he

mentioned her, peeking from under a thick towel to ask, "How many days are left before Mummy can come home?"

Clean, changed into flannel pyjamas, smelling of fragrant soap, the boys settle in the den for the hour (or so) of television they are allowed each school day. They record programs on TIVO, stored for this hour.

I have a palpable, almost acute, need to be physically close to my sons. I hug and hold them whenever we are in the same room. I leave the desk in the den and settle beside them on the couch while, half-minded, I review notes in the patient files I've brought home. Gathered around me, in the surprising, singular silence that television induces in young children, they watch an animated boy-superhero with a magic ring.

I am a devoted but insecure father. I have no sense of what I want to impart to my sons; no sense of what it should mean to them that I am their father.

The boys watch the television avidly, expertly flicking buttons on the remote control to quickly skip through commercial advertisements, quickly returning to hanging plot threads. It occurs to me, with some pride, that through this device, they have actually increased the value of their TV hour.

Looking up from the routine post-visit notes of a pregnant diabetic patient, I notice that the boys are watching an advertisement. It is a typical commercial. A woman returns from a shopping trip, steps out of a white minivan, and makes her way to the door of her home. Inside the house, her two sons and their father prepare for her return, arranging the living room. The father coaches the boys to give the right answers; they need to have been very good to earn the desirous toys the mother bears. Mother enters a house that gleams with order. Surprised, and suspicious, she questions each boy in turn. Then, in the same manner, she questions the husband. They answer in the same way, quick affirmatives, followed by quick nods of the head, like happy, gambolling dogs. Sceptical but generous, she dispenses, in turn, different versions of the toy to each of the boys and then to their father. The man and boys are overjoyed. The commercial ends with the camera panning up to disorder and clutter at the home's upper floor, a voice-over intones: "Dragits, the gift this Christmas for the boys in your life that have TRIED to be good."

I sense my irritation at the fact that this is the commercial my sons seem to have chosen to watch. I am aware at the same time that this reaction is not a rational one. The Dragits are often spoken of by the boys. It is clearly the gift they would each desire as presents at the end of the year. The commercial itself is standard fare on American television, the competent, wise wife, the

44

infantile, feckless husband, but I seem to have lost my ability to view it all with a wry, superior indifference. And this loss I can clearly trace to the moment two weeks ago when I had been having trouble with the sandwich grilling machine and my wife, bright-eyed and effusive from after-work drinks with some of her colleagues walked through the kitchen door and Ebitu announced: "Mummy, Daddy can't get the sandwich machine to work" and my wife, hanging her coat on the wall rack, her back turned to us, said: "Poor Daddy! Well let's just see if we can't sort that out."

When I have put the boys to bed, I walk down to the basement where, on an old desk, I keep the desktop computer on which I installed my dated practice management software. As the last bit of work before I relax completely into the evening, I come down here to enter annotations in the machine, reminders of what needs to be done the next day.

One evening, one of those rare evenings when my wife was at home, I had stayed down in the basement for what must have been an inordinate length of time. My wife, who must at some point have grown impatient, had come down to stand, in her night dress, at the top of the basement's stairs and called out an inquiry on why I was taking so long. "Are you watching porn?" she had asked, a pleasant, amused laughter in her voice.

"No, I'm not," I said, attempting to give my voice the timbre of irritated dignity. I closed the muted website streaming pornography and walked up the basement stairs.

Several weeks later, at a dinner in Baltimore with a number of my wife's former colleagues from her days at Hopkins celebrating someone's promotion (I don't now remember who), the conversation turned to the divorce of a physician who was well-known to most of those gathered at the small, Thai restaurant at which we were dining. (I had heard of him, of some renown in paediatric nephrology, but I did not know the man.)

The rumour, shared freely at the table, was that he was in the middle of a bitter divorce, triggered when the man's wife found a secret stash of pornography in their home. Around the table, there was some lazy speculation on the nature of the pornography.

Doug, a cardiologist, who, like my wife, has a postgraduate degree in public health, and who worked with her, also as a director, in the same international health institute, sloshed wine in an enormous wine glass and quipped: "It's true for paediatricians, as for all mankind, that only paedophilic porn is adequate grounds for a decree of divorce." I thought the quip a poor one, not worthy of the silence Doug had commanded to enable him utter it. But at the table there were many chuckles and I noticed that my wife smiled.

However, despite the laughter, many of the people at the table were uncertain of the validity of Doug's assertion and the opinion was shared by some that under certain circumstances: "Porn could be cheating." Cheating, of course, was grounds for a divorce.

At this point, my wife joined the conversation. She agreed with Doug and made the common sense observation that it was unlikely that porn alone was the reason for the divorce. As my wife spoke, I was surprised to realise that I felt an anger that made it impossible for me to speak or keep my eyes on her. The anger dissipated slowly and was almost gone by the time dessert was served.

I had, on several occasions, observed the little intimacies that passed between my wife and Doug. She would put her hand on his sleeve when she was making a point, for instance. And there was the evening when they had both said, almost in unison: "Just like in Indonesia."

Due to their positions, my wife and Doug often travelled together. Sometimes, Doug would drive her home from the airport and I would observe them speaking for minutes in the car parked outside our front door. One Saturday afternoon, on a day my wife and the boys had spent at the movies and the mall, I was surprised, helping my wife out of her white summer dress, to see the deep welts of fingernail scratches on her back. I was in that moment unable to form a coherent narrative to support what was before me and like one in a conjurer's show I appeared to myself to instantly forget what I had just seen. She did not notice that I noticed or perhaps she was herself unaware of the long fingernail marks. I said nothing.

These wisps, too transient and ephemeral to be formed suspicion, had in many ways permeated my being, and if I am honest, the single, irrefutable attraction of my wife's plan to move us all to Nigeria was that her co-employment relationship with Doug would come to an end.

I remember that the night my wife first mentioned the job in Nigeria we were lying in bed. I was reading a commando novel and she was on her laptop reading emails.

She described the position - as head of a new institute (amply funded by a hedge fund billionaire) dedicated to changing female health care outcomes in Nigeria - as a dream job. The pay tripled that of her current position and with the perks and allowances, she assured me, we would more than double our joint income. It was, she said to me, apparently without irony, the job she was born to do.

My wife achieved some early fame from the success of her first, and only, book: "Politics and Diseases of

Women in Africa." A slimmed-down, colloquial version of her Master's thesis, the book's primary argument was that the critical pathogen in the appalling disease rates in women in Africa is the skewed gender politics of that continent.

The objections, my objections, were delivered in hastily organised ambushes, as she made plans. What about the boys? What about my practice? Why do we have to move to another country? Neither one of us has lived in Nigeria in fifteen years!

Eventually, the objections began to appear, even to myself, hollow and shrill. And one evening, within the pretext of providing reasoned alternatives, I gave voice to my deep, unstated desire and asked, rather parenthetically: "You're a qualified physician. Why don't you open a practice or join a practice? We could double our income. There would be no travel and we would not have to move to god-forsaken Nigeria."

In that moment, her face lost its characteristic, ever-present air of cheerful amusement. "You are asking me to give up my dreams, to give up what matters most to me," she said.

• • •

When it rains at dawn in Lagos, the storm starts with the howl of the wind, then, for a time, the claps of sterile thunder. When the lightning comes, carving bolts in the dark grey sky, then, the rain comes. Hard and fierce, beating frantically on the roof. My husband sleeps through it all.

In the eerie grey gloom that ushers in morning, I walk through the upper floor of the large, colonial-era house that we now live in. The floor, made of wood, occasionally creaks beneath my bare feet.

The boys now have their own rooms. Arinze, my older son, is, invariably, the first to rise, hours before his ten-year old brother. He usually finds me downstairs at the dining room table, on my laptop, sending emails, making Internet calls to associates in the United States. Usually, it's my friend and ex-colleague Doug, who (annoyingly) has married a Filipino ophthalmologist and moved to the West Coast.

Arinze has a straight, proud back. He saunters into the dining room and, barely looking at me, impudently asks: "Who are you talking to this early morning?"

It's been four years since we moved back to Lagos. Four years and his accent has changed, taken on the hard edge with which the Nigerians here speak English. In the fall of every sentence, on the last syllable sits aggression, an accusation.

Arinze does not wait for an answer before he wanders into the kitchen. He is hardly there a minute before he calls out: "Mum, I can't find anything to eat!"

"Arinze, it's 5 a.m.!" I reply.

"I'm hungry," he responds.

I enjoy Arinze's directness, the assertiveness with which he confronts life. He reminds me of the way I was at his age. Except that I did my homework and got great grades. I had the third highest score in my primary school at the Common Entrance Exams. Arinze malingers at the back of his American International School class, pretends there is something wrong.

When we lived in Silver Springs, my husband spent hours helping him with his homework. "He is a bright boy," he would say, "he just needs to apply himself." Now, my husband's hopes are fixed on our younger son, with his excellent grades, his smiles, his passive-aggression, and cunning. For Arinze all he has to offer are silly jokes about the boy taking after my side of the family– a reference to my unaccomplished brothers. He avoids engagement with Arinze and his pre-teen problems. The solution my husband suggests is to send Arinze off to one of those ghastly Nigerian boarding schools, where, he says, "he can learn discipline."

Here we have staff. Maids, a cook, drivers. Yet it seems my attention is required for everything. I have to make sure the cook when making lunch does not put crayfish in the jollof rice (Arinze is allergic to crustaceans); that the maids wash the plates with sufficient detergent so films of oil don't build on our crockery. I issue instructions, make lists- grocery lists, task lists- for our unreliable domestic staff. I check for compliance. My husband floats through his day on a cloud above these domestic concerns, wafted aloft by puffs of "Good morning Sir"; "Yes, Sir"; "Yes, Sir"; from the genuflecting servants. When I suggest he might take some interest in what is going on in the house, he spreads himself further on our living room couch, folds his left foot under his thigh and asks me which of the servants I need him to talk to for me.

I have a busy morning. I had planned to leave early but when I walk out of the front door, Kunle, my driver, is missing again. I stand under the eave that shelters our front door from the rain watching the cook, a newspaper folded over his head, run off to look for him. The rain drums little holes in the soft sand, pushing dirt out of these miniature volcanos. I tap my right foot on the concrete doorstep. I am anxious.

The soft light and cool air of rainy mornings in Lagos conceal the nightmare of traffic that awaits, as if in ambush, at the first intersection. Cars swimming in the flooded streets, overthrown sewer rubbish floating at leisure, blasted horns, and the howling and hurled insults, the frayed nerves of people caught in a shared, repeating nightmare. I am eager to leave early and avoid its full brunt. But Kunle, my useless driver, has disappeared.

When he finally turns up, bowing in a repeated, insincere motion, "Sorry Ma!; I'm sorry Madam!; Sorry Ma!," it's almost 8 a.m. And I have to endure the rush hour traffic. Cars in motion, so jarringly close to one another that my initial instinct – since acclimated- was to flinch.

From the back seat of my SUV, I can see Kunle's profile as he pushes the steering wheel, muttering to himself, occasionally cursing other motorists in a low voice. I cannot stand the man. I turn away, looking out of the side window. There is a woman standing on the washed-out sidewalk. She is dressed in the tight black skirt and elaborately stitched blouse of the junior office worker. Her broken umbrella is held close to her side. She is thoroughly drenched.

I remember the night, when we were just married and I wanted to go to the rap concert after Howard Homecoming. He didn't. He didn't want me to go either, said it was unsafe. I left him at the dinner table, stewing over his rice, and went to put on my makeup. Later that night my purse was stolen. Wet and shivering, drenched in cold rain, I called him from a mobile phone borrowed from an elderly janitor starting a shift. He drove round to pick me up, wrapped me in blankets when we got home and left me to sleep. "If you like rap, you like rap," he said, smiling, when I started to mumble an apology. He was my harbour.

Over the weekend, I took the boys across Falomo Bridge to Lekki Market on an excursion to buy gifts for Kip and Carl, the boys' best friends in Silver Springs. When we set out, it was a stunning, sunny afternoon.

At the front of the market lay a line of concrete stalls, stacked with brightly wrapped, miniature, single serving packs of detergent, biscuits and instant noodles. ("This is lame," Arinze said.) But tucked at the back, we came across concrete stalls full of rusted, ancient rifles, statues, carved masks of wood and bronze, relics from a deserted time, ingeniously hawked to tourists and us.

When we left Lekki Market, an evening rain was falling, light and sweet. Arinze rode in the front with the driver, my younger son sat in the back with me, sleepy and quiet, his head curled on my lap.

When the boys were in bed, I wrapped the gifts in bright wrapping paper and put them against my husband's suitcase so he could pack it himself. (He had gone golfing mid-morning.) I got into bed with my laptop computer and turned off the light.

I feel alone here. It is a strange feeling in this city boiling over with people and life. I travelled out of

Nigeria a few months ago. I flew to London to give a speech at TEDx Euston. The event was organised around the thesis of development in Africa. I thought my speech, on health care improvement through small changes, was well received. I felt something of my former life in the exchanges with the bright-eyed participants and the question and answer sessions. I had to get back to Lagos the next afternoon, but that evening, sitting alone in a café drinking a black coffee, quietly watching those walking by on a street off Sloane Square, I felt a connection to my old self that was both sharp and surprising.

Weeks later, when the clip of my speech appeared online, a mutual friend of ours (I don't now remember who) posted it on his Facebook page. When I looked at the comments, I was surprised to see they were mostly my husband's friends. Most of them congratulated my husband, not me. His secondary school friend Kenneth tagged him: "Congratulations *enyi*, you have brought us a good wife."

(The first time my husband left our home at night without me, almost two years after we moved back, Kenneth knelt before me in our kitchen on a Friday night, charmingly asking me to "release" my husband to his custody for this one night. "He is a good man. I will bring him home intact." My husband flashed me a small, perplexed smile. Kenneth brought him home, drunk, at

4 a.m. Now, my husband goes out on Friday nights with a blithe announcement directed to the air and to me that he is going to meet his friends.)

My husband will be leaving today in the late afternoon for Murtala Mohamed International Airport. To catch a flight that will take him back to Maryland. He is on his way to Silver Springs, where he plans to sell our home. My husband was the one who insisted on holding on to it, renting it out at a subsidised rate, just in case we needed to come back. Now that he thinks we should sell, I find I have nothing sensible to say.

I won't be home before he has to go to the airport. His flight is at midnight, but with the traffic, and now the rain, he will have to leave the house before 5 p.m. to catch it.

As we get on McPherson, the traffic barely moves. I get out my phone and call Ronke, my assistant. My early appointments will need to be rescheduled. While I am on the phone, I feel it buzz with an incoming call and, momentarily, I pull the phone away from my ear and look down at the caller. It's Dayo Amaechi, an acquaintance and occasional companion. I continue the conversation with my assistant. When I get off the phone, I see Dayo has sent a text message. It's long and chatty, at the end she asks if my husband and I are available for dinner on Saturday. I put the phone aside.

The last time we had dinner at the Amaechis' was over six months ago. Dayo had served soup and some sort of duck dish that she seemed very proud of – she even brought out her French-trained, Beninoise chef to take a bow (and a small round of applause).

Her husband, Chike, a large, deep-voiced man, playfully teased her about this: "Your mates are boasting about the egusi soup they cooked with assorted meat, you are bringing out Cordon Bleu chef to take bow." He was clearly taking great pleasure in his wealth and the fact that it purchased his wife such indulgences. My impression, formed over the few occasions we had socialised with them at dinner parties and the one night we had stayed over at their beach house off Tarkwa Bay, was that he wasn't a bad guy and there was something in that deep baritone that suggested depth.

After dessert was cleared away, we moved to a living room that overlooked their magnificent pool. Chike walked around the room, offering cigars from a squat humidor to the men. When I said I wanted one, he turned to my husband and said: "I like this your wife."

I turned to his wife and said: "You have such a lovely home."

"Thank you. Chike did most of the designs," she replied.

"I heard you wrote a book," Chike said.

"It was written many years ago, but yes, I did," I said.

I then started to tell them about the book and also about the work of my institute. At some point I said: "The sheer level of bare-faced sexism even among educated Nigerian men is appalling."

"Ah, ah. We are not that bad," Chike said, smiling.

"It is that bad. And it is not a joking matter. This is a chauvinistic society. It is simply perverse," I said.

"Please, please, stop! Don't bring this your American women's lib nonsense here," Chike said.

"Chike, mind yourself, that's somebody's wife," said another of the guests, a tall man wearing glasses.

Chike turned to my husband and said: "My brother, I beg no vex. Please, caution her."

And my husband laughed, clearly enjoying himself. "Why should I caution her?" he said. "She is telling the truth." Then he took a long draw on his cigar.

Angrily, I bark at Kunle: "Didn't you see that car! What is wrong with you?!" I decide in that moment that I will sack my driver – for the second (and final) time. When I first fired him, over a year ago, he turned up at my husband's office with his two wives and a clutch of children. They had come to beg.

He said the man and his wives threw themselves on the ground between him and his car as he was leaving the office in the evening, pleading in woeful wails. "The man is the sole provider for that motley brood." My husband asked me to reconsider. And because I remembered one of Kunle's wives had written me a thank you note (touching in its atrocious syntax) for a small gift I had given his family for Christmas, I reconsidered and rehired him.

Now, when my husband and I get into the back seat of the SUV and I tell Kunle where we are going, I notice the missed beat, while he seeks my husband's face in the rear view mirror for confirmation. Once, soon after Kunle was rehired, when I asked my husband if he had noticed this behaviour, he said he hadn't and suggested I was perhaps reading too much into the situation. "Maybe he is just checking that you aren't kidnapping me," he said, and smiled.

The grey clouds are lifting and the sun, in Lagos always forceful and direct, strikes the back of the moving cars. The traffic is beginning to ease up. The hawkers start to emerge, large tin trays perched on their heads. I hear something familiar on the radio. Right then, my phone starts buzzing. I ignore the phone and ask Kunle to turn up the volume on the sound deck.

Piano and guitar chords and the voice of Elton John singing Rocket Man fill the car. "I miss the earth so much, I miss my wife" and then, later: "Mars ain't the kind of place to raise your kids." Something about the song brings back to me the experience of driving at night on

Interstate 95, the headlights cutting into darkness, street lights throwing off a pale glow, passing at a rate steady as a metronome's, rest stops flooded with neon light, approaching and receding in the distance; something in the song makes me miss America.

Christian Mothers

I come upon the small village slightly after noon. The sun is hot. A dusty earth road runs through the village. Beyond the road, lined with dirt-brown buildings, wooden doors and rusty zinc roofs, lie forested hills of fervent-green grass and leaves. The road ends where the village ends, at St. Charles Parish Church. The taxi stops at the entrance of the sandy driveway of the Parish Church to let me out. Then turns and drives off in a cloud of dust. I walk up the driveway.

Teenage boys cut at the tall grass beside the Church with thin cutlasses. They work in squads, sweat slicking off their arms and backs as they land their strokes in unison, working to a beat. An old woman is climbing a ladder leaning against the Church's side wall. Her feet are bare.

The boys pay no attention to the old woman. I stop to watch.

The woman gets to the roof and removes her head scarf. It's a strip of blue cotton printed with repeating portraits of Pope John Paul II. Each portrait is framed by a rosary, and the Pope's fingers are raised in benediction. She ties the scarf around her waist and then screams.

The boys stop their work.

"Uwa agahi ezuru anyi. This world is too small for Agnes Nwadike and me! Either she will have to leave it, or I will leave it for her." The old woman threatens to kill herself by jumping off the uneven roof of St. Charles Parish Church, Umudim.

Cutlasses still in hand, the boys gather around the dirty, dusty walls of the church. From a distance, it looks like they are her pursuers, as if the woman has climbed up the roof to escape them. I set my bag down and sit on a large rock in the shade of a trumpet tree whose branches stretch over the driveway.

The boys aren't fools. They know that if the woman really wanted to jump, she would have jumped already. Some of them say, "Please, Mama, don't jump." They are perhaps kinder, stronger, or more sentimental than the other boys who mock and taunt her, saying: "Jump, old woman!" Though they are joking, I sense it is their instinct that the old should die.

The boys are glad for the excuse to leave their chores. They laugh, happy for the unexpected entertainment.

The boys' jeering and loud laughter cause the women of St. Charles Parish Christian Mothers Association to end their meeting. They come through the church's front door in groups of two and three. The women are all dressed the same: a blue head scarf with pictures of the Pope, a white blouse sewn with frilly, lace-like material, and a blue cotton wrapper around their waists, cut from the same Pope fabric as the head scarf.

The noise is now loud and contentious. Different voices rise and fall. Some women plead, "Biko, come down," just as some scold, "You are a disgrace. Look at how you are disgracing us! What have we done to you!?" Some of the boys jeer loudly to call attention to themselves, "Has this old woman gone mad? But if it is madness, she would have jumped," and others shout in louder voices to call attention to their wit, saying, "What she is doing, what is the difference between it and madness?"

I reach into my bag for a small bottle of water.

A lone woman emerges from the church and looks up at the roof. She is dressed like the rest. One of the other Christian Mothers walks up to her. "Agnes, Agnes!" she calls. She grabs Agnes by her elbow and points to the barefoot woman on the roof. "Clementina says she will kill herself because we elected you head of Christian Mothers."

Agnes is silent. Her shoulders fall in defeat. "This is how this useless woman has stolen my day of glory," she says. "Nobody will remember I was elected leader of Christian Mothers. All anyone will talk about is this useless woman."

Agnes walks among the other Christian Mothers, trying to persuade them to continue the meeting. Clementina's cries grow louder as Agnes speaks to the Christian Mothers in small groups of three and four. "I am going to jump! You people have killed me! When Father comes, don't lie. Tell him you killed me." The cries seem to have their intended effect. The other Christian Mothers stay outside, shouting, "Stop this nonsense!" None of them goes back into the church.

Agnes's mood shifts from resignation to anger. "Please, stop filling my ears with noise," she spits at the other women. "Let her jump," she hisses and walks back into the dark church. "What a useless woman," she shouts as she passes through the threshold.

I sigh. This will be my new parish. Umudim is very much like my own village. The village I left to join the seminary and become a priest. Umudim is just as dusty and bare, with nothing but dirt-brown houses, a small market, and a parish. The Christian Mothers clean the church every first Saturday and Sunday of the month. They prepare food on a schedule to feed the parish priest and also, on a schedule, clean his house. These women are like my mother and her friends. They are alone. I know. I have been to other parishes. I have seen these fights before. The interminable feud of villagers who have no one else to punish. The women spit a lot. It is an instinct to let the bitterness out of their mouths. The sons they once built their lives upon are gone. The young men leave the villages for Lagos, Port Harcourt, or Aba. The old ones die. I close the water bottle and put it in my bag.

Suddenly, some of the boys scramble onto the roof. Clementina shouts at them, warning them not to come any closer. A few Christian Mothers urge the boys on. "Grab her, grab her tight." The boys stay where they are.

The noise quietens. The teenage boys are getting bored. One of them suggests that they go and fetch the parish priest. Another agrees. The tallest boy on the roof slides down the ladder and takes off in a sprint. He is wearing dark blue shorts. He hesitates as he passes me at the entrance, then takes off in a full run. His shorts are tied to his waist by a piece of red cloth. He is not wearing a shirt. He is not wearing shoes.

Everything slows down around the church as if a foreman has called a break. Clouds pass in front of the sun, casting shifting shadows that slowly dissipate. A white, rusty Volkswagen Beetle drives up to the front of the church. Father Ignatius hardly stops the car before he jumps out, angrily screaming at Clementina. He turns and beckons to me. The bottom of his white cassock is brown with dirt from the burnt-red earth.

"What are you doing?! Have you gone mad?" Father Ignatius continues screaming at Clementina. She seems surprised at the priest's vehemence but does not reply. Turning to face him, she makes her way down from the roof. Some of the boys help her. Her feet, dry, dusty and scaled, touch each rung on the ladder. She tries to suppress a smile as the Priest continues to scold her.

"Agnes started it," she protests to Father Ignatius in Igbo. "Okparir'm. Agnes insulted me. She told me, 'Don't be silly'. Muwa? Me? It's me she is telling 'Don't be silly'?!" Clementina sings the English phrase 'Don't be silly' like it is a single word. She walks away from the church building.

Agnes emerges from the church door. The other Christian Mothers gather around Father Ignatius, each trying to tell him what happened. He ignores them and starts ordering the boys back to work, calling some of them by name. The teenage boys snicker and giggle as they start to move away. The sound of their cutlasses cutting at the long grass resumes. Soon, a beat is established. I see the tall boy in the blue shorts stroll up the driveway and join the others cutting grass.

Father Ignatius extends his hand, and I shake it. "They told me you would be here tomorrow," he says in English. "Let us go inside." He then turns to the women. "Christian Mothers, look at how you are disgracing all of us in front of the new Parish priest." Then he adds in English, "All of you go inside."

I stand at the door with Father Ignatius as the Christian Mothers enter the church. "These women are always fighting. If it is not one thing, it is another," Father Ignatius says. "Especially that Clementina Azuonye. She is always at the centre of any fight. When food is being shared at an event, she will threaten to overturn the big pot of jollof rice unless they meet her demand for extra pieces of chicken." Then he laughs.

"I tolerate her, though. Her son is at the Vatican. He is a Monsignor, a cardinal's private secretary. Her husband was a highly respected primary school teacher. He died a few years ago. Since then, she has gotten worse." Father Ignatius walks into the dark church. I join him. Light and noise filter through the half-open door and windows.

Father Ignatius begins his meeting with the Christian Mothers. I step outside and wonder if I should risk a cigarette. Then, I see Clementina Azuonye peering in through one of the church windows. "Nne biko," I call to her, "please come."

She walks over to me and, placing one hand on her hips, asks, "Are you the new parish priest?"

I confirm that I am. "Welcome," she says, "I hope you won't be like Father Ignatius, always taking the side of that stupid Agnes Nwadike." I tell her I will not be on anyone's side. "I hope so," she says, and then sneers "Don't be silly!" in the same sing-song tone.

"That is what my husband liked to tell me. 'Don't be silly'. When our only son announced at eleven that he would be a priest, I laughed. I expected his father to talk sense to him. He is an only son. He needed to marry early and have many children. Instead, my husband encouraged him, talking nonsense about sacrifice to the Church is the highest honour." Clementina pauses, and her eyes dart from side to side. Her face is gaunt, the skin tight and worn. "When I started shouting out to the neighbours, summoning them to come and hear with their own ears the evil that was befalling me, my husband ordered me back into the house. He told me, 'Come on, don't be silly!'" Clementina sighs, then spits on the ground.

"I am sure you are not an only son," Clementina says. I tell her I have three older brothers. Then she looks up at the sky, slowly shaking her head as if in regret. Her scarf is still tied around her waist. Her hair is short and tangled with many clumps of grey. She stops shaking her head and then focuses intently on me. Her head is still, like a person focused on a distant sound. "Wait, let me go and hear what they are plotting," as she starts to creep back towards the open church window.

Using the light from a kerosene lantern, I arrange the spare room in the parish priest's house. I will stay here for about a week before Father Ignatius leaves for his next assignment. The room is small, but it does not matter. I do not have much in my bag. The rosary my mother gave me when I left for the seminary, my transistor radio, and my copy of The City of God. I hide my pack of cigarettes under the mattress. My mother was the head of Christian Mothers in our village. She was respected. Everyone called her "Nne Father." When we came home to bury her – my eldest brother, who sells second-hand clothing in Kampala and my two elder brothers, who are in the same business in Aba, only thirty-eight miles away from our village – this is how everyone referred to her, Mother of a Priest.

I learned from the transistor radio that Pope John Paul II had died that night in Rome.

Father Ignatius introduced me to the congregation the next day after Sunday Mass. I make some general comments and then announce His Holiness' death. The church is quiet for a moment, and then impromptu prayers are offered by several voices for the soul of the

Pope. Father Ignatius imposes order by saying a formal prayer. After he is finished, Agnes Nwadike stands. She calls for an emergency meeting of Christian Mothers at four o'clock that Sunday evening. Clementina Azuonye stands up to object to the proposed meeting time.

The Naming Ceremony

We *are fragile things*. It is a strange thought to have at a party but tomorrow is the naming ceremony of Kunle Ogundipe's first child, and he is feeling philosophical. The music in the club thumps, and purple shafts of neon light pass rhythmically across their faces. The tall waitress is leaning down, her legs bent at the knees, gathering glasses and champagne flutes from the low table. "They send the beautiful waitresses to the VIP," Kunle says, speaking to no one in particular. Akin looks at the waitress with a curl on his lips.

"It doesn't look like Otunba will come," Akin says.

"Well, I certainly didn't expect him," Kunle says.

"Abeg, abeg," Akin retorts, his voice gravelly with irritation. "You know I know your father better than you." Kunle looks at Akin.

"No, seriously," Akin continues, "I got Otunba to your bachelor's eve party. I know how to talk to the man. Don't be a bastard."

"A bastard is a man with no father, you bastard," Kunle says in an even, flat voice. Akin stares at Kunle.

"More champagne, ladies?!" Akin shouts to the seven young women he gathered for the party from the University of Lagos. The prettiest stands up, raising her champagne flute. Her lipstick is pink. Kunle leans against the velvet-red upholstery of the banquette, pushing his back into it.

The champagne comes in buckets - each bucket held above the shoulder by a waitress in a black dress. A waiter- also wearing black - walks behind them with a fistful of sparklers in each hand. A herald, the DJ changes the music. To a song with a strong beat and a simple chorus: "Pop! Pop! Pop Champagne!" The girls in the VIP dance, hopping up and down at each "Pop!"

Akin jumps on the banquette with a champagne bottle, hopping up and down on one foot, the other raised in a high step, his face fixed with a broad grin. Kunle sits quietly in the corner. He has not moved.

Across from the entrance to the VIP stands another low table. On it are a few shot glasses, a couple of Star beer bottles, and a half-finished Fanta bottle. Around the table are five women who look like they are guarding it. From a distance, in the low light, they seem fashionable. They are wearing second-hand clothes.

The pink lipstick girl watches Kunle like he is a prize. "Those girls are prostitutes," she says.

"And you are what?" Akin says with a nasty sneer on his face.

"Abeg," the girl replies, turning her face away, "who is talking to you?"

At 2.15 a.m., Kunle and Akin walk out of the club. The night is sharp. Akin has his arm around the waist of the girl with pink lipstick. Kunle walks alone. The street glistens like dark skin with sweat.

"Chairman! Omo billionaire! Son of a rich man! We are here for you. Always loyal!" Startled, Kunle looks down in the direction of the voice. A man with no legs and a wide, manic grin is pulling himself astride Kunle, perched on a short wooden board with wheels. The man's head barely reaches Kunle's knees.

"Rich boy!" It's another voice. Another legless man on wheels rolls beside Akin. Behind them, four legless men are frantically paddling with their arms, trying to catch up with the young men.

Kunle continues the walk to his car. Akin stops and throws some money at the legless men. He pretends to kick one of them. They sing out praises, "Omo baba 'lowo!" Kunle looks back. The legless men raise their arms in salute. They wear rubber slippers on their hands like they are feet. Akin walks to his car, accompanied by a

73

troop of begging double-amputees. His right hand rests lightly on the buttocks of the pretty girl with pink lipstick.

The naming of a child is to be done on the eighth day when it is certain the child has come to the world to stay. The ceremony should be performed at dawn to seal the child's compact with its naming day.

In memory, he knows his mother is coming to him. He is five or six years old. He is in bed. He has been sick with malaria. Fitfully sleeping away the day, accosted by delicious hallucinations. Bats that hover with un-flapped wings, like levitating rats. A coiled python that wants to be his friend, speaking in a high, girl-like voice.

He can hear his mother at the front door. "How is Kunle? Is he better?" He can hear her footsteps approach his room. He is filled with delicious anticipation. He cannot wait for her to come to him. Her jasmine perfume, to him, is the scent of sweet, soft, clean things. He anticipates the smooth, cool feel of her flesh.

When she opens the door to his bedroom, he closes his eyes and pretends to be asleep. She sits on the bed, kisses his cheek, and places the cool back of her hand against his forehead. He can smell jasmine- sweet and clean things.

"Has Kunle eaten?" Bring This, Bring That, she calls to the maids, not leaving his side. He opens his eyes. "Mummy. Funke." She smiles. He feels a thrill. He has called his mother by her given name. She shifts her weight, puts his head on her lap. Soon, he is asleep again.

"Where is your husband?" Bolanle asks her sister.

"He went to Kunle's party. I haven't seen him since he left," Funke Ogundipe replies.

"That is what he told you?" Bolanle says.

"Maybe he ended up at one of his guest houses. Why are you worrying yourself? Otunba won't miss his grandchild's naming ceremony."

"I can't understand why, in heaven's name, you've started calling him Otunba. And I could care less if he makes it to the naming ceremony," Bolanle says. There is a pause. "It won't be the first one he has missed."

There is a long silence. "He likes to be called Otunba. It's his title." Funke says, "He's earned it."

Bolanle lets out a loud, derisive hiss. "You are pathetic," she says.

It is 6.30 a.m. The sisters are seated on a cushioned bench in a large ornate foyer with a marble floor, waiting to leave for the naming ceremony. They have been drinking tea from white, gold-rimmed, porcelain tea cups embossed with strings of pink roses.

"How did you get here?" Funke asks.

"That's a silly question. I drove," Bolanle says.

"I know you drove. Did you come with a driver?"

"No, not all of us have a chauffeur at our beck and call," Bolanle says.

Funke smiles again. Bolanle does not respond. She sips her tea and then says: "I don't know how you continue living with that bastard. How can you even stand to look at him?"

Funke's smile disappears. "Please, let's go. Don't bring trouble to me this morning."

"I am not bringing anything. I am asking you how you can live with the man you call Otunba," Bolanle says.

"Stop, please," Funke says quietly. "It was my fault."

"Why?!" Bolanle screams. "Why is it your fault? Because you had an affair? How many affairs has he had?!"

"I don't want to cry," Funke says, tears gathering in the cup of her eyes.

"You are the one that is crying," Bolanle says. Then she hisses again.

The women walk outside as dawn rolls into a new day, leaving a fringe of orange in the low clouds. Delicately, the two sisters settle into the Mercedes limousine's back seat. Their elaborate gold geles touch the soft ceiling of the large car.

The honour of naming a child is usually given to the head of the family, its patriarch. Usually, this is the child's grandfather or great-uncle. When this is not done, the child is named by its father.

This also is in memory. His father has asked him to his office. He is ten or eleven years old. He is frightened. He doesn't know why he has been summoned. He doesn't know why he is scared. His father has never hit him. His father has never yelled at him. But he has seen him yell at others. He has seen him hit others too.

He has to climb the second set of stairs outside the house to get to the office. His father is behind a desk in a leather chair. Light pours into the room from a window behind his father's head. It makes it difficult to see his father's face. All he sees is the outline of his father's head, framed against the light.

His father is holding something out to him. He cannot see what it is. His father waves his hand, up, then down, gesturing for him to take the object. "Quickly, Kunle. Be lively." When his right hand reaches for the proffered thing, he realises it is a tightly-tied brick of Naira notes. More money than he has ever seen before. He stands before the desk, confused, the bundle of notes held tentatively with both hands in front of his body. "Should I give it to mummy?" he asks.

"No!" His father shouts. Then, there is silence. He cannot tell what his father's eyes have fixed upon. He still stands before the desk. He can feel time passing.

"You are my son," his father suddenly announces. "You are the man in this house when I am not around. Don't depend on any woman, not even your mother." His father leans into his desk. Now, he can see his father's eyes. They are fixed on him. "I know a child will always love its mother, even if she is a prostitute. But don't depend on any woman."

He doesn't speak. His father is silent. He stands before the desk for a while. Then his father tells him to leave. "I want to see how you handle money," his father says when he is almost through the door.

The black limousine drives up to the white gates, which swing open quickly, pushed by two enthusiastic men wearing grey uniforms. As the car pulls up to the entrance of the white house, a man in a flowing, white agbada strides toward the car and jumps in with a small, theatrical hop.

"Have you selected a name?" the man in the white agbada asks the large man seated in the limousine.

"I have Dolapo," Otunba Ogundipe replies, "but the first person that will hear the name is my grandchild."

Dolapo laughs. "Aburo, I thought you would be late."

"Emi? Me? Late? It is not possible," Otunba says.

"That young woman's eyes! She was looking like she intended to teach you a lesson."

Otunba chuckles. "It's the girl that you should have been worrying for. It is not today that I started handling women. I tell these young girls that what their small boyfriends will show them twenty years from now, I can show them today."

Dolapo laughs.

"Your own is too much." Dolapo shifts in his seat and adjusts his agbada. "And you are lucky. Funke is such a good wife. If I stay out the whole night like that, my wife won't let me have peace in this house again."

"It is you people that are pretending to be good."

"It is not pretence, o. I am good. Especially compared to you, Otunba!" Both men laugh.

It is tradition for the father to keep the child's name a secret, even from their mother. This tradition is now rarely observed, and it is common practice for the couple to confer.

It is a posture, a pose, fixed in memory. The children stand against the front grille of their father's new car, waiting to have their picture taken. He is seven or eight years old. The car is black and shiny. They have been arranged against the car by someone in birth order or by height–it is a time when both still mean the same thing.

He comes first, then his sister Atinuke, then his younger sister Muyiwa. Someone is missing. He wants to tell the photographer to wait. But the light bulb flashes. Then they are rearranged. He cannot see the person who is doing the rearranging. He is placed in the middle. "Kunle, look at the camera." Put your arm around your sisters. Smile. It is his father's voice. But he can't see him. He can hear the cameraman laughing. Now, he can see his mother beside the cameraman, wearing a white dress with large pink flower prints, laughing. The cameraman is not his father. The man with the camera is tall, with a beard and glasses. He is smoking a pipe.

His father is not here. Perhaps it is his father who is missing? The man with the camera starts laughing. He does not know why the man with the camera is laughing. His mother starts laughing too. He does not know why his mother is laughing. Then he starts laughing too.

"Should I take it as another sign of your deep and, may I add, irrational suspicion of your father that you have me

researching Yoruba naming ceremonies on the Internet?"
Toyin asks her husband as she adjusts the computer on
her lap.

"I don't put it beyond these people to just make up
something and stuff it down our throats. They will tell
you it's tradition, and you, like a fool, will just believe,"
Kunle says.

"Well, so far, it's checking out," Toyin says, peering
at the screen.

Kunle is cradling their sleeping child against his
chest, pacing their bedroom floor. "What time is it?" he
asks. "People will be here soon."

"The priest is already here," Toyin says. "And there
are a few guests downstairs. Once your parents get here,
we start."

The baby is sleeping. Kunle is rubbing its back.

"Your sisters called last night when you were out.
Apparently, it's freezing in Boston." Toyin says.

"If they don't like it, they should come back to
Nigeria. It's warm here," Kunle says. "What else did they
say?"

"Just to wish us good luck for today." Toyin pauses.
"Atinuke says we should call the baby Omotunde – The
Child has Returned. She said you were convinced you
had a missing brother. When you were children."

"I don't remember ever telling her that," Kunle says.

"Well, she said you did. She always thought you wanted a brother." Toyin is not looking at Kunle. Her eyes are fixed on the computer screen as she speaks. "She says now, in a way, you have one." She smiles. "I like Omotunde. We can call him Tunde. That's a nice name."

Kunle smiles. He crosses the room to where his wife is seated, bends over and kisses her forehead. "I honestly don't remember telling Atinuke that. But I do have a memory of a baby. I am two years older than Atinuke, and she is barely two years older than Muyiwa. It can't be them. Strange. My mother says it must be my imagination."

Toyin looks up at her husband. "Maybe she lost a child and didn't think you could handle it. Maybe she couldn't handle it. Have you asked Auntie Bolanle? Have you asked your father?"

The central ritual of the naming ceremony provides the child with a taste of the world. This, of course, is done symbolically— by giving the child a tiny taste of the Seven Things.

What he remembers is clear and sharp, without shadows. He is eight or nine years old. They are in the aisle of a well-lit supermarket. He is pushing a shopping cart. His arms are raised above his head, so he can reach the handlebar.

His mother walks ahead of him. She is holding on to one of his sisters with each hand. The shelves are high. His mother stops and turns to look at a shelf stacked with green cans. She calls him, "Kunle, bring the cart over here." She lets go of Atinuke's hand. As she stretches to reach for a can, he sees it clearly. She is monstrously pregnant.

In his mind, he is not surprised. But he cannot hold on to this image- his pregnant mother reaching for a can of sweet yellow corn. Like pictures from an erratic projector flashed on a wall, this image is abruptly replaced with that of his pregnant mother furtively eating flesh off a bone by the light of an open refrigerator door. It looks like a chicken drumstick. Of her lying on a couch, tiny liquid beads on her brow, her face turned to look vacantly through large, glass sliding doors. What ties these images together? His mother is not smiling. Also, the scent of jasmine is missing. What he smells is like worry, a smell like sweat.

It is then that the shadows come. The grocery store is no longer bright in fluorescent white. A single bulb throws yellow-brown light on the aisle. Atinuke takes off running, and his mother calls out her name.

He can feel things lurking in the shadows. He does

not know what they are. He tells himself that they are night cats. They can see in the dark, and they eat rats.

It is 7.10 a.m. Two women are standing outside Kunle Ogundipe's house. One of them smokes a cigarette.

"If it is me, I would have poisoned him," Bolanle says. She is speaking to Stella, a large woman in a gold gele stubbing out a cigarette with the toe of a crimson pump.

"And if she poisoned him, who would have paid for her children's education?" Stella asks, "Where would Kunle, Atinuke and Muyiwa be today?"

"I don't care! I would have poisoned him." Bolanle says. "What kind of wickedness is that?"

"How do you even know Otunba had anything to do with it?" Stella says.

"Stella, stop talking nonsense! You are a lawyer. I spent the night with Funke preparing for the naming ceremony. I saw it with my own eyes. They didn't look right. They didn't look left. They walked straight to the bedroom, picked up the baby and left the house." Bolanle says.

Stella looks down at the cement paving stones. Two cigarette stubs are on the ground, their tips smeared with lipstick. Stella lights another cigarette. She turns her face. The smoke does not reach Bolanle's face. Bolanle stares at Stella, with her palms resting on her hips, in a fighting stance.

"He let her carry that baby for nine months, and all the time, that was what he was planning?!" Bolanle's voice is low as if she is speaking only to herself. "You know when he confronted her, Funke said she would get an abortion?"

"I know. Funke herself didn't know whose child it was."

"He let her carry that baby just so he could make her suffer." There is a pause. "He is walking around, and you people are calling him Otunba."

The two women are silent. They look at each other, suddenly uncomfortable in their shared company. Stella blows some more smoke.

"When he came back to the house that morning, do you know what he said? Everybody is crying. We have policemen running around the house asking stupid questions. Funke is hysterical. And this bastard saunters into the house and asks, 'Did you people finish the naming ceremony without me?' Right there in front of the Assistant Superintendent of Police."

Prayers are offered for the child as each of the Seven Things is placed in its mouth. The first four, the sweet things, are:

Omi (Water)—*That the child's life shall be calm, cool, without trouble.*

Iyo (Salt)—*That the child shall have zest in its life.*

A'adu (Cornmeal mixed with oil)— *That the child shall always be nourished with savoury things.*

Oyin (Honey)— *That sweet things shall pervade the child's life.*

When he looks back, this is the way he remembers happiness. He is the first to see his father. He is six or seven years old. His father is speaking to a man in a uniform at the entrance of the large hall. The man is nodding and waving his father through. His father drops to his knees. He is laughing, and his arms are held wide open. He is running into his father's arms. In his father's embrace, held tight, he can hear the disjointed female voice announcing the arrival of British Airways Flight Something-Something from London. Passengers may pick up their luggage at the carrousel in the E Wing.

His father is carrying him in one arm; the other is wrapped around his mother. His father is kissing his mother - her lips, eyelids, and shoulders. He is touching her cheek with the palm of his hand. The carrousel turns. They are waiting for their luggage.

Then he is riding his father's shoulder, and his father carries Atinuke with one arm. The other holds his mother's waist. His mother is carrying Muyiwa. Muyiwa is small. So small that sometimes he forgets her. They are pushing their way through a crowd of people.

He knows they have been somewhere cold. He has seen snow. He has worn overcoats and gloves. But even now, that memory is fading. The cold place is shifting, unreal. He remembers now getting on the plane. He remembers the plane starting to come down from the clouds, so out of the window, he could see the sun and the zinc roofs with brown rust. The large logs on the lagoon look like matchsticks floating on dirty oil.

He has fallen asleep. He wakes up in the back seat of his father's car. They must be heading home from the airport. Atinuke is asleep beside him. His father is driving. He can hear him laughing. His mother is telling his father something. She is smiling as she speaks. His father reaches to touch his mother's face. He feels warm. Then he falls asleep again.

"Mommy, please, I can do it," Toyin says to her mother-in-law.

"Toyin, let me help you. What am I in the world for if I can't look after my child's child," Funke says.

"Mommy, your grandson is lucky. I am lucky. We are all lucky to have you," Toyin says.

Funke smiles. "You are very sweet Toyin. My son married well."

Toyin smiles. They turn the baby around. Together they work to remove the cotton clothes and slip the white baby caftan over his head.

"Is Kunle treating you well?" Funke asks. "I know he can be moody. Sometimes he stays quiet like he is fighting the world. Don't let that bother you. It's just the way he is."

Toyin smiles. "Things are much better. He is treating me well. He's been in a very good mood since the baby was born," she says.

"A child brings joy," Funke says. She is playing with the edges of the blue baby blanket. Her eyes fixed on the tufted strands. Toyin watches her quietly.

The baby starts crying. Funke looks up. "Ok! Let's go downstairs. This one is ready," she says. Toyin picks up the child and holds him to her chest.

"I think he is hungry," Toyin says. "Let me feed him before I bring him down."

Funke Ogundipe gets up and leaves the room. Tears are in her eyes when she gets to the door. She wipes them off.

Downstairs, the living and dining rooms have been arranged for the ceremony. The dining table has been moved to a corner, covered with a white tablecloth. The

Seven Things are laid out on the table, on the expensive American Atelier Sicily Blue Dinnerware Toyin bought for a different purpose. Two carved, straight-back chairs have been placed behind the dining room table.

Ten or eleven people are in the room. There are many more people outside, where a white canvas canopy has been erected. Under the canopy, white plastic chairs are arranged around white plastic tables.

Akin walks into the living room behind his wife. "Let me go and look for Kunle," he says to her. "Otunba wants to talk to him." Akin's wife barely turns her head. She keeps on walking.

Kunle is standing with the priest and an old man wearing a faded, tie-dye caftan. The old man speaks in Yoruba. "You can't just name the child. It is not a dog. You have to find out how it came into the world. What path it took. Every child comes with a purpose," he says.

Akin walks up to them and whispers into Kunle's ear.

So, it may know the world, after the child is fed a taste of the sweet things, it is given a taste of other things. These are:

Obi (Cola nut)— That ill-will, bad luck and illness is expelled from the child's life with the same life-instinct that causes the child to puke at the cola nut's bitterness.

Orogbo (Bitter Cola)— That the deep healing of bitter

medicine stays with the child, and it lives a long life with lasting health.

Atare (Alligator Pepper)— That the child has passion, hot, like the alligator pepper and that passion begets children, numerous like the alligator pepper's seeds.

He remembers that the night was dark. There were three of them, huddled in a crouch below the fence. Akin is in front. They are fourteen or fifteen years old. They are in boarding school. They are attempting to get out. They have done this before, to drink beer and smoke cigarettes. This is different.

The house is not large. It is long and narrow, with many small rooms on a long corridor. Cloth lines crisscross the corridor. Wet T-shirts, underpants, and bras dangle above their heads. Some still drip. Akin stumbles out of the room. It is now his turn.

"Are you ok?" the other boy asks Akin.

"It is the girl you should be worrying for," Akin boasts. "It's not today I started this business. Turn by turn. Kunle, oya, it's your turn."

The room is dark. A single incandescent bulb is hanging from the middle of the ceiling, throwing off a small yellow light. He can smell a stink, like old, stale sweat. But there is something else, a sweeter stench, the aroma of festering, fermenting things. There is a small, low wooden bed in the corner. On the bed lies a bronze-skinned woman. She is wearing a soiled, nylon chemise.

"Small boy, come and do quick," the woman says. He is startled. He moves closer. The chemise is a light pink, with two dark stains on the left side. The larger stain spreads to the woman's navel.

He starts to remove his trousers. The woman sits up on the bed to receive him. He shuffles to her.

Nothing happens. He can feel nothing. The woman plays around with him. It makes things worse. He can feel something awful rising within him. He feels disgust. He does not know why he does it. He does not know when he does it. He can remember it only as something he has done. Suddenly, he has called the woman: "Ashawo! Prostitute!" He has spat on her face and is running for the door. He feels a thrill. She hurls a tin cup at his head. It catches him on his ear as he is almost through the door. They all take off. Running as fast as they can. In the night air, he can breathe. He feels clean.

Otunba Ogundipe is seated on a wide, cream couch in Kunle Ogundipe's home office. It is a small room with a small orange rug. Dolapo is sitting beside him. They have just been served tea. The waitress walks out of the room and closes the door behind her.

"Dolapo, you are my friend. I want you to witness

what I will say to my son and how he will answer me. My hand is clean with that boy," Otunba says.

"Kunle is a good boy," Dolapo says.

"He is quiet, and he is meek. Akin leads him around. At least the Akin is vigorous, even if he is a bit rascally," Otunba says.

"Kunle has his mother's quiet nature. It is not necessarily a bad thing."

"Dolapo, I have suffered at Funke's hand. Please stop praising her near me," Otunba says, adjusting his position on the couch.

He is leaning forward towards his friend. "Kunle takes from me and pretends that it is not him that has received. Instead of coming close to me, my son acts like it is not me feeding him. Is it his salary he used to pay for this house? That girl he married, would she look at him twice if not for my wealth?"

"Aburo, I am sure the boy appreciates," Dolapo says.

"What he does not understand is that everything I have is for him. What else am I working for?"

The men are quiet. The sound of the humming air conditioner fills the silence. Dolapo starts drinking his tea. Otunba is leaning back, pushing his back into the couch.

Suddenly, Otunba starts speaking again. "Funke disappointed me. It is not something I can describe. The love I had for that woman…" His voice trails off. The room is quiet. Very quiet. Then abruptly, he starts again: "Do you know what it feels like to look at your wife and know…" Again, his voice fades. Dolapo holds on to the teacup. He is sipping carefully. Putting the cup between himself and Otunba's eyes.

"Do you know what sacrifice is?" Otunba asks. "Wait. Don't answer quickly. Think of what I am asking you. Do you know what sacrifice is? Not just the one of a fetish priest. It is in the bible. Abraham and Isaac. When they say, for this, you have to sacrifice this, or you have to sacrifice that, what is it that they are talking about?"

There is silence again and the hum of the air conditioner. Dolapo puts away his teacup.

Quietly, Otunba continues. He is speaking slowly. "There are things you need to do. Things that kill you. But they are things you need to do as a man. I've kept this family together. I sacrificed for them. Kunle, Atinuke, Muyiwa. Even Funke. I sacrificed myself."

"Aburo, aburo," Dolapo says gently, placing his hand on his friend's knee. "What do you want to tell Kunle?"

There is another silence. A long silence. It is broken when Kunle knocks at the door.

After the patriarch, or the child's father, has pronounced the child's principal name, the name is sealed by dropping a coin in water.

Others may give names and seal these names by dropping coins in the same water.

The child is named Olusanya Omotunde Ogundipe. Olusanya means God has compensated me for my past suffering. In keeping with tradition, it is Otunba Ogundipe that chooses the name. The old man in the tie-dye caftan beats on his talking drum. The drum, in its ancient language, with syncopated beats, praises Otunba Ogundipe. He showers the drummer with crisp Naira notes.

When the naming ceremony ends, breakfast is served under the canvas canopy. The DJ starts playing music. People dance.

We are fragile things, Kunle Ogundipe thinks.

A Line of Fold-Up Chairs
and One Pastor

It was the sound of clanging brass cymbals, ringing
through the light dust of the harmattan haze, that
brought Chuka to Pastor Anozie Moses. And it was
Pastor Moses who brought Chuka to the lean-to church,
to Jesus, and to a short-lived conviction on the possibility
of human salvation.

He called out to him. Chuka was taking a shortcut
through the Boys' Quarters – the low, stout building that
stood guard over his parent's backyard— through the
clearing with always-wet, green grass and a large open
drain.

In this clearing, during the work week, two large
women set up competing open-air restaurants around
squat wooden tables covered with thick plastic sheets
festooned with purple and rust-coloured flowers. Their
helpers - girls really - heaped enormous mounds of rice

and beans onto brown plastic plates. Their customers - men mostly - sat on benches, a few in dress shirts and ties, eyes fixed, carrying laden spoons to their mouths. The cooking was done in large, blackened cauldrons, under a lean-to, beside the drain's restraining wall.

But it was a Sunday. The clearing was almost empty. A few men and a woman with two gangly children gathered around the deserted lean-to. Chuka wasn't paying attention.

"God's blessing, my brother! Praise Jesus!" Pastor Moses called to him as he walked by. "Come worship with us. Na my church be dis." Chuka could see no church. Pastor Moses stood beside a line of white fold-up chairs, a bible in his hand. Chuka ignored him and kept walking. "Thank you! Thank you!" The pastor called after him, "God bless you, my brother."

This also became routine. On Sundays, on his walk out to the beach, to Kunle and Banigo; to the late afternoons when Alero came and listened to him play his guitar, holding her hair and smoking a spliff, as the sun was starting to set over the Atlantic and the clouds were riveted with shafts of purple and yellow light, and the ocean water was just beginning to rumble. On Sunday afternoons, before all this, Pastor Moses would call out to him.

Chuka knew the type. These men of God. From

when he was sixteen, in the depths of his trouble. When his mother would drag him off on Friday, Saturday and Sunday evenings, to some cavernous steel and concrete prayer hall for All Night Prayer Vigil and get him down on his knees, gripping his hands, screaming, "Praise the Lord!" And he thought: what shit.

Pastor Moses is the oldest elevator operator. His elevator is the cleanest, and the one summoned to bring the Managing Director down from the Fourteenth Floor. Once the Managing Director adjusts his tie, Pastor Moses flips the override switch; this is an express ride. "Pastor, how are you today?" asks the Managing Director in his blue, too-tight, bespoke suit. The Managing Director is in a jocular mood. Pleased with himself. Pleased with the contours of the world as it rests on him. Pastor Anozie Moses is in uniform. A blue overall, with the badge of his employer – a shield guarded by prancing unicorns- sewn to his chest.

"God bless you," the Managing Director says as he leaves the elevator.

"Thank you. Thank you, sir," Pastor Moses replies. Instinctively, he feels it presumptuous to ask God's blessing for the Managing Director.

As the Managing Director turns the corner and the

elevator doors begin to close, the Pastor hears a call, "'Old it, 'old it!" A middle-aged woman in a black suit jacket half-runs to the lift. Pastor Moses recognises the woman. Eighth floor, an accounting department supervisor who is always eager for the Pastor's view on the everyday coincidences she is convinced are portent. He holds the elevator, and she steps in. They are joined by three men in light shirts and dark trousers going to the eleventh floor.

The elevator is lined with aged, chipped Formica paneling and in a corner is an ineffective, rasping fan. It squeaks to an imprecise alignment with the eighth floor's granite landing. Pastor Anozie Moses has not finished his explanation. He holds the door open.

"You see, my sister, that is the way God works. The reason is that God wants to use you to touch her. I don't know how many of us have seen God. Have you seen God any day?" Pastor Anozie Moses looks around the elevator's cab with a daring, knowing confidence. "Have you gone out one day, seen God, and said, 'God, good morning?'" There are a few chuckles. "That is not how God works. God works through you."

"Pastor na true you talk. God bless you, my brother," the eighth-floor woman says as she leaves the elevator.

Pastor Moses smiles.

"God bless you, my sister," he calls after her.

It is almost 5 p.m. Closing time. Then the mad rush for the elevators- the pushing, the jostling, and the loud refusals to step out of the overfull cab when Pastor Moses commands. The young executives in suits and ties slyly mock him: "So you just sit on that stool all day pressing the buttons?" And then quip, with a condescending smile: "If you weren't here, there would be room for one more person."

This is the time for him to gather his things. The bible, the old radio with an improvised antenna of thick electrical wire, the copy of his employer's last Annual Report, which he carries to and from work for no discernible reason, and then his purple thermos flask.

He carefully packs these things into the synthetic-leather bag he keeps wedged between his elevator stool and the lift's back wall. Soon, it will be time to walk into the Men's Toilet and put on his preaching suit.

On weekdays, before the impromptu traffic-light motor park; the clanging metal of bus doors on rusted, motor oil-black ruts; before the shouts of bus conductors, leaning out of slowing buses: "Obalande! Obalende!"; before the ride on the small danfo bus where you sit, cramped and bent as if to puke; before the ride on the large bus (packed, so sometimes you cannot sit) that will take him over the Third Mainland Bridge (while in traffic, the sun sets over the lagoon); before the four hours (on four buses) that will take him home; before he can set his back to the Devil and the doubt that creeps into him, carried by the wisps of foetid waste seeping from the pores of fellow travellers. Before all this, Pastor Anozie Moses puts on his preaching suit.

A black suit, five-year-old now, made by an itinerant Togolese tailor to Pastor Moses' detailed description of the Managing Director's pinstripes. Even down to the red inner lining that added three thousand naira to the already dear cost. The Togolese tailor had taken liberties and Pastor Moses' description was imprecise, so the suit is perched between styles - odd-fitting. It is this suit that Pastor Moses wears back and forth, to and from work, ministering to the flock in buses. It is this suit he wears on Sundays.

As the large bus crawls onto the Third Mainland Bridge, Pastor Anozie Moses lifts his arm in a powerful salute. "Deuteronomy 2:7: For the Lord, thy God hath blessed thee in all the works of thy hand. All the works of your hand! Then why are you failing?! Something is behind it. Locate your prophet." He turns to face the back of the bus with a slight smile on his face. "There are demonic forces, and there are keys to unlock them. False prophets will perform false miracles. Are you getting it? Don't be fooled by them. God never does any miracles for show." Pastor Moses turns to the front of the bus. "Am I communicating? Are you getting it?"

"Sit down, my friend! Stop making noise!" a man shouts from the back of the bus. Pastor Moses is used to hecklers. "Thank you. Thank you, my brother," he says, "Maybe it is you the Devil has decided to use today. You must be vigilant. You must fight it."

"God punish you!" the man at the back of the bus retorts.

There is some laughter. Then the bus and its exhausted commuters fall to silence.

On Chuka's bedroom wall, the one that runs alongside his bed, is a large poster of Jimi Hendrix, with a scarf around his neck, a joint in his mouth and a finger on his lips.

On weekdays, Chuka tries to keep still. Tries not to make the noise that will attract his mother's attention. Bring her stomping up the stairs, peering through his bedroom door, slight hesitation, weariness perhaps, and then again, The Speech. Go back to university. If you don't want to go back, get a job. And on those rare evenings his father is home, by the television watching NTA news, swallowing eba balls, pretending to ignore his wife scolding his son; on those rare evenings, his mother raises her voice and flows into the story of his father's heroic struggle with poverty. The university degree and –in a straight line progression- measurable fortune, all earned on just sweat.

Chuka looks at her and tries to be still. Words— words that contest or words that acquiesce— words prolong. And he wants it to end. So, he keeps his lips still even as he thinks she leaves out that his father's fortune was made on over-inflated contracts, half-profits kicked back to his father's cronies at the Ministry of Defence. Every change of government brings palpable anxiety to their household. Who will be made minister? Will the Lieutenant-General in charge of the army be removed? Who is close to the new president? Who will be probed – payback for political errors? When governments change, his father will wear his white agbada and follow his mother to All Night Prayer Vigil. He convenes nightly family prayers with the indignation of a colonel who discovers his standing orders have been neglected. And once- when it was his father's contract that was probed- assembled an army of prayer warriors in the front yard to intercede on his behalf, in tongues.

As his mother speaks, Chuka keeps his mind outside the room, his mouth shut. He imagines the world in which he lives, the house in Lagos, on a cul-de-sac near the sea. As if telescoping in reverse, drawing back, he imagines all the other people in Lagos, in Nigeria, in the world, on a blue planet circling the sun. He thinks everyone is on this rock, hurtling at terrific speed in dark space. It seems to him that this is an important fact; this is the thing everyone around him ignores. This is a large ship with no navigation and no controls. Everyone is a passenger. There is no way to get off. No one knows what will happen. No one even knows what could happen, he thinks. He imagines men all over the world - men like his father and his father's friends who get up in the morning and strive after something. He imagines that these men, in their hearts, want to be elected Ship Captain. With guns or bombs, or bribes, they want to dictate where the ship will go. These men don't seem to realise what appears blindingly evident to him. They can't become Ship Captain and can't say where the ship will go. They can't even say how their own lives should turn. Even if they became more powerful than any man has ever been, all they could ever be is Cruise Director. The buffoon in charge of entertainment. Like that girl Julie on the Love Boat.

He starts to smile.

"Do you think I am joking?!" his mother shouts angrily. "When your father kicks you out of this house, don't come and beg me. Idiot!"

But Sundays are different. On Sundays, he can wait

until his parents have left for church, then lunch at the Radisson or Sheraton, and then a wedding, funeral, or engagement ceremony. On Sundays. they are gone the entire day. And on Sunday, he goes out too.

Alero comes out to the sea on Sundays. Plays with the coloured bangles on her arms and laughs, loud gurgles that echo like waves between the stones. And sometimes she sits close to him, slips her fingers in the mass of his tangled hair, leaning her head on his shoulder. And Chuka looks out on the sea, and Alero, and he is certain the sensation of her hand on his spine is what keeps him together.

As they sit on rocks, the brown sand between their toes, Chuka sees the dark-skinned, bare-chested Rastafarian who sells weed approach. The man crouches beside them, presenting a painted wooden board with necklaces and bracelets hanging on rusty nails. "Buy something for your babe. Respect the African queen. Respect."

"How much?" Alero asks, running a wooden necklace through her finger. She laughs when the man names his price, drops her hand into her bag and pays the vendor half of what he asks.

"It's junk," Alero says.

"Why did you buy it?" Chuka asks.

"It's pretty, too," she says and smiles.

And Chuka smiles as Alero pulls his head into the crook of her arm.

Pastor Anozie Moses walks into the parlour of his small, three-room flat. He can feel the sweat drained from him pooled in the armpits of his white, second-hand shirt beneath the fabric of his preaching suit. Through the day, he has kept a tight hold on his thoughts, wary of where his mind could lead him. It is not thought he has feared. He fears the thoughts that lead to feelings. The feelings that can betray him. He fears the feeling of loneliness. The one that undoes him.

"Pastor *nno*. Uncle, welcome." It sounds like the two things are said in unison, but he can hear the split-second timing. His fourteen-year-old niece has been faster, her eleven-year-old brother a bit slower but warmer.

"God is good," he replies.

"All the time!" they chorus.

It is now that he releases his hold on his thoughts. Only with these two, who grab to help him with his synthetic-leather bag, escort him to his room and wait outside the door with his rubber slippers while he takes off his preaching suit, pulls on a white cotton singlet and ties a faded, wax print wrapper around his waist.

Unusual for a man his age; he is not married and has

no children. His sister moved in with her children six years ago after her husband abandoned her.

"Brother, come and eat," his sister calls out through the door of his room. He can feel his grip tighten on his thoughts and then his feelings. His sister's presence sets his mind slightly off, at an angle. Her presence, a dull, rusty edge that would have been imperceptible to him during the day - in his work overalls or preaching suit - now jars at him in his home.

They eat sitting on a raffia mat on the floor of the parlour, the one of his three rooms that leads out to the world. The other room is his, the third shared by his sister and her children. The cooking is done outside on the ground floor, on a wood fire beneath raised red bricks under another lean-to with a corrugated zinc roof. The bathroom and toilet are shared with the other three flats on the tenement's second floor, down at the end of the corridor, away from the stairs from which light rises in a shadowed arc to the landing.

On Pastor Anozie Moses' parlour wall, the one beside his old television set, is an enlarged, framed copy of the change-of-name newspaper advertisement.

"I, formerly known as Anozie Amadiora, now wish to be known as Anozie Moses. All previous documents remain valid."

The formal words, publication in small print in the

right newspapers, along with documents attested to at the right High Court and filed in the right ministry. A new identity. It is dated almost five years ago when he had the revelation that his last name- Amadiora– was a fetish name, unacceptable to God.

Beside the framed newspaper announcement is a large piece of cardboard, yellowed, designed to look like an ancient scroll, centred behind the television. Printed on it: "God called unto him out of the midst of the bush, and said Moses, Moses. And he said, here am I. – Exodus 3:4."

"Leave the dried fish alone," Pastor Anozie's sister says, hitting the upturned palm of her daughter's hand. Pastor Anozie looks at his sister. There is a warning in his eyes. He picks up the dried fish, divides it in two and gives one piece to his niece and the other to his nephew. His sister says nothing, turns her head and fills a plastic cup with water.

He knows why she says nothing, does not shout at him or spit in his face. Because she is completely dependent on him. As his church has grown, his income has grown. He knows this is why she comes with him to his church on Sundays; drags behind him on Saturdays when he goes door-to-door to spread The Word.

When they were children, she was an unreliable ally, quick to betray him for any advantage. He understood why. He can feel the draining rush even now. The acrid, slow-burning air of a home without love.

When the evening meal is finished, and his sister has carried away the serving dishes and the brown plastic plates, he gathers his niece and nephew, gets them down on their knees, and prays. He prays for their upkeep, for their protection from temptation, prays for triumph against the machinations of evil spirits, and then, for the longest time, he prays for the success of his church.

After prayer, the best part of his day. He sits with his niece and nephew, and they talk. He asks them about school and about their homework. His niece earned a distinction in biology. "Praise God! May his name be blessed!"

Then he tells them about his day. "You people will not believe it! The church is growing. It is amazing how God is working. I have always said that one day this church will be as big as Pastor Oyedepo's church. Even with branches overseas." There is a look on his niece's face for a split second. The look of disbelief. Pastor Anozie's difficult life has made him a watcher of faces. He sees the look and forgives. He continues: "I know people are laughing at me, is such a thing possible. But yes, it is. God blesses who he wants to bless."

"Praise the Lord," his niece and nephew chorus.

"Can you imagine that, even now, people are looking at me overseas? That young boy from my office, Reginus, who came to the church. Do you know that he filmed me when I was preaching with his telephone?" He looks at the two children with a smile at the sheer wonder of it.

"They are now watching it in America! Do you children know what is YouTube? I was on YouTube. The boy in the office was showing me. I was so happy to be watching it with him on the Internet. And this other guy in the office was asking me 'Moses, Moses is this you?' And I said 'Yes, it is me.'"

At midnight, Pastor Moses concludes he cannot sleep. Surprisingly, the electricity has still not cut out. He sits up on his wood frame bed, clears his throat, and then reaches for the lamp switch. Electric light, delayed, floods the room. He places his foot on the brown-red linoleum flooring that covers only half the room.

It takes him a moment to focus on what has been holding him from sleep, unsettled. It is the story some men in the office had told him of the pastor whose congregation had come together and bought him a plane. A private jet.

Pastor Moses has never actually been on a plane. The idea one had been purchased for a pastor unsettles him. He wonders if his congregation could soon buy him a motorcycle. Who knows? One day, maybe, even he could get a plane. Involuntarily, he smiles at the thought, turning his palms upward and pushing his arms slightly forward as if passing the responsibility to God. His arms open, ready to receive.

He had asked the young men who had told him the story how much a plane costs. They had mentioned widely differing numbers, and he had concluded that they did not know.

He is not anxious. His church has significantly increased his income, and it is growing. He reaches into the synthetic-leather bag for the small notebook in which he keeps an account of his receipts. With a yellow pencil, he starts summing the numbers.

One Sunday, instead of coming out to the beach, Alero dies. On a plane that falls to the ground, on a bright Sunday when the sky is blue and the clouds white and puffy, like they were made for babies to play with.

And Chuka opens his mouth, and the salt breeze and the froth of the sea rush in. And he expects a howl. But he is quiet. The sounds are held-in, denied to the world while tearing away at his viscera, at those organs whose real purpose is to sustain life, not muffle screams. And the world itself is quiet. And he floats in that absence of sound that shocks those whose ears are close to a terrible blast when all sound converts itself to an image. Slow-moving, phantasmagorical things that wander around with more substance than ghosts.

And Chuka walks, dazed, through weeks. Picking at his guitar strings, ranting on chat rooms and Facebook, throwing his MacBook down the stairs, the expensive machine dropping hesitatingly step after step in the wake of the mother who has come to him to say: "Don't use this as an excuse."

And as time passes, Chuka can sense the edges of what he feels. And it is an absence. An absolute absence. And all the yearning in his heart is also for absence. He wants things to end. And on certain days, when he is alone in his room, he says to himself: I Feel Like Dying. And this sounds awful to him. Grotesquely false. As if someone has occupied his body, someone stupid, thinking nonsense.

Soon, it is his father who comes up the stairs. He looks into Chuka's room, but he does not make a speech. He comes with common news, things you might read in a newspaper, things he imagines Chuka might think interesting. Sometimes he hesitates at the door when he is leaving. He always says "Good night" and "See you tomorrow" before he shuts the door.

And on another Sunday, life continues. Pastor Moses calls out to him. And Chuka stops. And Pastor Moses raises his bible with a big, friendly smile, his lips chapped by the dry harmattan wind. There are a few beads of sweat on Pastor Moses' brow. Chuka, trying not to notice, notices the sweatbands seeping over, staining Pastor Moses' collar, the fraying, cheap polyester tie, and the yellow-brown shirt cuffs.

"My brother, thank you! God bless you. Finally! Eh, today is wonderful. Wonderful. I've been telling them one day Guitar Boy will come," Pastor Moses gestures behind him towards his congregation and laughs.

The gathering is larger. A small, square canvas canopy has been placed against the lean-to. It is a rental, taken down after the Sunday service, the metal tubes that hold it up clanging as they are thrown on the flatbed of a rented truck.

Pastor Moses seems ecstatic. "You see, my brother, God wants us all to be happy. He wants us to prosper. He has made you answer me today. Can I get an Amen?" Pastor Moses is smiling. Chuka looks at the pastor. Chuka isn't smiling. He looks like a person that might cry.

Looking past Pastor Moses, Chuka's eyes have fixed on a gangly girl helping a tall, dark man tie two cloth banners to the top of the canvas canopy. The first reads: "God's Battalion Miracle Church. Pastor Anozie Moses." The second, now unfurled, reads: "Put to death what is earthly in you. Colossians 3:5." Chuka recognises it-from somewhere else.

And something about it makes him think of Alero. Perhaps because he believes it's what she would never say. And then he cannot stop. Alero is in his mind, picking up her large raffia bag, turning to Banigo and Kunle, who are arguing about nothing, in that way they have of talking about nothing, stringing echoes of meaning. Alero is saying, "Later, dudes," putting her arm around Chuka's shoulder and hugging him from behind before walking through the door.

Chuka's tears finally come. Slow, large and wet. Quickly flicked away. Pastor Moses lays a palm on his shoulder. "It shall be well my brother. God is in control."

And Chuka moves away from his touch and walks past the banner, under the white canvas canopy, into the lean-to church. The gangly girl reaches for his hand, leading him, as one might a very old person, to a fold-up chair in the front row. Beside him, a gangly boy beats a tune on two drums. The boy's eyes are on Chuka's guitar. The boy varies his pace, drawing up and letting go.

Chuka places his guitar on his knees and starts to strum, accompanied by clanging cymbals and drums. The music is beautiful.

And the following Sunday, Chuka sits up early on his bed and looks out of the window undecided. He pulls his guitar off the wall, and frets. And still unsure, he pulls out a white shirt, black tailored trousers and a navy blazer he has not worn in years and lays them on the bed.

He walks through the dining room, where his parents are still having breakfast. And his mother, amused, asks: "Where are you going dressed up like that?" His father says: "Leave the boy alone."

And he walks through the back door, past the Boys' Quarters through the clearing and into the lean-to church.

And Pastor Moses' God's Battalion Miracle Church grows.

Love and Other Masquerades

When I was a girl, the gloom of Okija's night sky discomfited me. By the time the sky turned from a mass of purple to the deep darkness almost impervious to the occasional light of kerosene lanterns, I had retreated to the bed at the corner of my room, praying that I would fall asleep and not wake until dawn. This was not the universal reaction to the night. At least not in my father's house.

While I retreated to my bed and the hope of sleep, my father's other children would gather around their mothers on raffia mats, seated, their legs straight out, sometimes holding hands, sometimes clapping, listening to their mothers' magical stories.

In my bed, the stolid darkness was imprinted by my mind - as I tried to see through it- with shadowy, shifting shapes of congealed blackness. It echoed for me the stories that were told by mothers to their children.

Stories of evil spirits that sprang through the night, blowing out candles and lanterns, accosted the dawdling child that had let dusk meet her on the slippery, craggy path that led back from the stream, and broke the water pot on her head.

I dreaded the night. And although I grew out of girlhood and learnt many things. Learned, for instance, that there are tender things that thrive only in darkness. The night sky has continued to hold for me this fundamental terror.

"Eucharia! Eucharia!" my voice echoes through the hall. She is always late, half-prepared. When she appears at the door, I ask: "Where is the soap?"

I don't have her run a bath often. Perhaps six times a year. Eucharia often forgets the steps. Her hair is in a tight plait, in a style similar to those worn in the village of my youth. She gets on her knees and vigorously stirs the flakes of bathing soap into the huge bathtub. Her wrapper comes undone. Her sweat-stained T-shirt– 'Ihejiani '07' – is from the last election campaign of our current governor. My husband, watching the governor's inaugural speech, had turned from the television in disgust and said: "An animal that should be in the zoo, they've brought out to rule human beings."

When Eucharia leaves, I untie my robe, let it drop to the floor and slip my body into the bathwater. The momentary sight of my body in the misty mirror, as it often does now, shocks me. Who is this old woman?

I no longer linger in front of mirrors or enjoy the fleeting pleasure of a chance reflection off a glass door. Now, when I sit in front of my dresser mirror and put on make-up, I do so quickly, trying not to notice the deepening wrinkles and folds.

I know you hear this and laugh. What complaints can I make about beauty and age? My limbs, skin, and the bones in my cheeks that held your gaze these decades have also held their own in time.

But ageing can only be deferred. And now I have aged past the point – in my fifties and sixties – when young men occasionally held my eye in a daring stare. In acknowledgement, I suppose, of the beauty they saw I once had. Now all anyone can see is an old woman. A handsome, flaccid, old woman.

Yes, you always teased me about my beauty. Teased me gently, generously, like the casual worship suitable to a self-conscious god. I can almost hear your chuckle: "You are a god now? Goddess, I don't blame you, o."

It was always your smile, your smile and your laughter. Your teeth, white, broad pillars, open behind the drawn curtains of your large generous lips.

The first time, on the last night of the African Judicial Officers Association's annual meeting at the Hilton in Cairo, you pulled the sheets that covered me away from the bed. "I want to see you. I want to see all of you. Whatever happens, whatever this life brings to me, I will always have this," you said. You stared and I, self-conscious, drew you to me. And then your right arm wrapped around my waist, and I moaned.

I was lying in that bath, thinking of these silly things, when one of our daughters called through the door to tell me you had died. "Mummy, mummy, did you hear? Uncle Chike is dead." And I lay in the bathtub, the warm water lapping at me, and stared out the window.

Sometimes, after the rains and the harvest, my father and his eldest son Okike, my half-brother, would slip away in the middle of the night. From my bed, I would hear them walking the path from our family's compound, humming a guttural, frightening hymn, the night eating up their words.

This was before the war, when men still went out to the forests at night. When my father's wealth was at its peak, and he did business as a produce merchant, buying up the work of farmers and loggers to sell to the trading companies.

I would lie awake in bed, listening, through the regular calls and wails of the night- the shrieks and hoots of beasts, bats and nocturnal birds- for the ominous sounds of men and their spirits.

When I think back, I cannot remember ever hearing my father and Okike's return. But they always did, and everyone acted as if they had never left.

It was from one of my half-sisters, the youngest child of Okike's mother, that I learned the purpose of the trek into the night. "Okike has been consecrated in the Mmanwu guild. He knows the Mmanwu, the spirit of the dead, and the Mmanwu know him," she boasted. One of our older sisters quickly shushed her, warning that the Mmanwu would come and carry her off if she kept babbling.

On those awful nights when the Mmanwu ran shouting and shrieking through our village with voices alternating between a cruel and frightening base and a loud, high-pitched wail, I curled up in my bed, even though I knew my father and brother Okike were in the night running with the Mmanwu.

I am very patient with the house cleaning now. It surprises me that I can still do this well. Eucharia is more hindrance than help. I try to restrict her to the sweeping

– and of course, anything else that requires stooping. To clean well, you have to remember all the steps to make sure you cover everything. But in the middle, I can only think of how my body turns towards you and your hands on my hips.

Your funeral is today. I won't go. Everyone around me, it seems, is going. My husband said he couldn't miss it. For a moment, I searched his face for malice. There was nothing. He meant only that everyone else is going. It is what he ought to do. He is going with one of our twin daughters.

My husband is a fastidious man. He has always been. I help him brush lint off the dark grey suit he has chosen for the funeral. He is examining the black shoes he will wear. Our houseboy Clement has polished it to a shine. Still, my husband scrutinises it before he judges it adequate and reaches for the long shoe horn. I help him knot his tie. Black and textured, it stands out against his white shirt. Even now, at his age, I know he will be the most elegant man at your funeral. It amuses me that this would irritate you.

He has flourished in retirement. When he ran Unilever, the function of the office and his ideas of what they required of him constrained him; boxed him in. Now, he spends his time playing golf and painting watercolours in his den. The years of the boardroom, and the politics, when he stood in the way of your fuel supply contracts or whatever your fights were about, are behind him.

You mocked him. "He is like an Englishman, so prim and proper and so condescending. I am tempted to tell him some home truths," you would say and laugh as I lay with my head on your chest. And I would laugh with you.

I thought you said these things because you thought I would never leave him for you. But then you never asked.

Obiageli, our daughter, comes into my room with her phone at her ear. She is talking to someone at her child's school. Her voice is raised, harsh. When she gets off the phone, she smiles. She has gotten her way.

The younger of the twins, she is your copy in face, build, and character. So obvious to me that it always baffled me that everyone was oblivious. Initially, I was terrified that one day someone would blurt out what I imagined everyone else must have seen.

In those early years, when you would stop by the house with your wife and son for the twins' birthday party and Obiageli would call out to you, "Uncle Chike. Come and see," her arm raised above her head, beckoning and you would scream "See what?!" laughing loudly and walking to her, my heart felt like it would jump and stop.

It was not until the girls were about nine that I lost that terror. They looked even more like you, especially Obiageli, but by then, I had realised that no one would see what no one wanted to.

Obiageli is now divorced. She lives openly with her boss, who has never been married and appears to have no intention of marrying her.

Obiageli tells me it's none of my business. We fight all the time. It started when she was a teenager and has never stopped. Even when things are good between us and we laugh and chat, she is wary, as if with a sworn enemy with whom she must be careful not to drop her guard.

She has come to tell me that she is going on holiday with her boss. She wants to drop her son off for the fortnight. "The nanny and cook will come and stay for the two weeks. My driver will take him to school and back with the nanny. You don't have to do anything."

I don't dare object.

"Where is Daddy?" she asks and goes to find my husband in his den. I can hear them laughing when I walk past the open door. He is seated on the couch. She lies with her head against his chest.

It is my husband who insists that I go to visit your wife. You have been buried for a month.

When was the last time I saw you? How many decades have passed since I saw you naked, your chest heaving in anticipation? Yet, since you died, I have lain in the bed I share with my husband, and I have thought of you every night.

One night, I dreamt of you. We were at a cocktail party. We were still young, in our forties, and you wore a bowtie. Even in the dream, I could feel your arms, feel that I wanted you to kiss me and then make love to me.

Why has there been so much time and room in my life for you? Even when my life was packed with trials and chambers, the girls' after-school piano lessons, shopping and errands, there was always time to drive to a hotel room you had reserved. To take off my wig and gown or business suit or evening dress or gele and wrapper and let you make love to me. There must be a reason. Do you know why, now that you are dead?

At breakfast, while I am telling him about the calla lilies I want to plant on the walk to our front door and Clement is pouring him a coffee, my husband tells me that the right thing for me to do is to go and see your wife. He says it is understandable that I was not feeling well enough to attend the funeral, but now that time has passed, I should stop by and take something over to her. Our families have been close, and our children grew up together, it must be a massive blow to your wife. I should visit, he says.

I flatly refuse to go.

My husband doesn't argue. "We share each other's grief. That's what friendships mean. Especially now." He shrugs and starts to cut his eggs with a fork and knife.

How long were we lovers? A decade, perhaps? Before and after the twins were born. It is difficult now to know. Difficult to understand what to count. There were so many breaks. So many starts and stops, and a lot that was unclear even in between. It is the end that is clear. That crazy year, when the girls were about seven. I was schizophrenic, nearly mad with the longing for you and the face I needed to maintain to keep my home and life afloat. The year when I would neglect to pick the girls up from their ballet lessons because I craved a few more hours in bed with you. When I could barely look my husband in the face. Not because I was afraid or ashamed but because I feared he could see the hate and contempt for him that filled me up to my eyes. Hatred and contempt solely because he was the vile creature that stood between you and me.

But of course, even then, I knew that was not true. Nothing stood between you and me. Just you and me.

The gardener has dug up dirt to the left of the front walkway. Clement has put out a lawn chair, so I can sit and watch the work. I select lilies for the gardener and watch him bury them in the soil. I always loved the feel of wet, clayey dirt between my fingers. But now, my gardening is limited to giving instructions and any pruning I can do without having to bend too much. Sometimes I kneel to weed or plant, but someone needs to help me get up. It is an uncomfortable, helpless feeling. I avoid it by asking the gardener to do the planting and weeding. I watch him so that it's done correctly, but also so I can feel it's still my garden. The clouds are gathering, drifting into the face of the sun and casting odd shadows on my flower beds. I think it will rain.

Do you remember the weekend we spent in Calabar? When it rained, it seemed, for every minute. We never left the hotel room. You would order room service and glance out the window and say, "It is still raining. Good thing we have nowhere to go," before you met the server at the door and took the tray of food from him. On the second night, after we exhausted ourselves on the enormous hotel bed, you said: "This one is for the highlight reels."

Through those years, in those many hotel rooms, my favourite time was when I was getting ready to leave. I would pull a skirt on, snapping on a brassiere or buttoning a blouse. You would be lying in bed, content, asking me questions about my day, why I had to leave you right away, why I couldn't stay longer. Sometimes you would ask why I couldn't always stay with you. But always, you would try to seduce me again. Kissing my back and neck, running your fingers up my thigh as I tried to get dressed. Sometimes it worked, and I would stay another hour or two; sometimes, I left, but that was always my favourite time.

And it was in one of those moments, the twilight between staying and going, that we stopped being lovers. It's been a long time, but I remember clearly. My lips bled.

I don't remember the hotel. But I remember how fragile I felt. Like my life was collapsing into a vortex of longing for you. A black hole, elongating and stretching everything into a string of nothingness. As I buttoned my blouse and slipped on my wedding ring, you pulled on my hand and asked me, "Why do you have to go? Let's stay here forever." I sat down on the bed and asked you. Yes, not clearly, jumbled in tears and incoherent words. But you must have understood what I meant: "Why won't you just let me go?"

"Why would I ever let you go?" you asked and smiled a broad, cruel smile.

I hurled words at you. Angry, nasty, bitter, words. We never spoke. Not like this, not about anything. Our words, your words, were always wrapped in laughter, light-speckled things that only hinted at meaning. I was demanding to leave, and you held on to me, asking me to calm down. Then I spat in your face, the glob sliding from your nose and cheeks to the edges of your lips. You struck me across the mouth with the back of your hand.

There may have been more between us after that night. I remember you sent flowers, boxed gifts and profuse apologies, but I am sure that was the night it ended for me. Not the longing. That never ended. Giving in to the craving. That was what ended.

The cries of the Mmanwu were muffled by night. I was almost asleep, but the shadows of my mind followed the low sound moving stealthily through the forests and farms of our village. Suddenly I rose in fear. The sound got louder as if it had given up pretence. It was a piercing guttural sound, loud and timbered, right outside our compound. Everyone in the household was now awake.

The children and wives clambered to windows to see what was going on. The bravest of my siblings went outside. I looked out through one of the windows at the masked spirits. The three Masks were bellowing my father's name. Two were as tall as two men put together, and the third was as short as a dwarf. The Masks were covered by what looked like raffia straw except for their wooden faces, which glowered with red, burning eyes and strange beak-like noses. The dwarf Mask seemed impatient. He had what looked like a smouldering pot on his head which would ignite whenever he started pacing.

My father responded from inside the house in a loud voice. "Who is calling my name?!" His voice was clear and sharp. He had not been sleeping. He sounded like someone who had been waiting for a summons. The Masks said nothing. The dwarf paced even more impatiently and then started calling out my father's name in a sing-song, almost mocking way, varying its calls with my father's various titles.

My father was outside the house now. He stood straight in front of the Masks and again shouted, "Who is calling my name?!"

"Nwadike, it is us that are calling you. Do you know why we are here?" the dwarf bellowed. It had not stopped pacing. The tall Masks swayed like whirling tops bolted to the ground.

"Ahu Akunna, how can I know why you are here?" my father responded.

"An evil thing is brewing in your house. We do not know its father." The dwarf Mask had stopped pacing, but the pot was still on fire. And seemed to get hotter, with smoke and flames flaring as it spoke.

"Ahu Akunna, I hail you. What kind of evil thing

brews in my house?" my father asked in a quiet clear voice.

The dwarf Mask started to pace again as if my father's words had infuriated it. "Nwadike, Nwadike, Nwadike!" it bellowed, "Do you presume to question a spirit?"

"Ahu Akunna, I dare not."

"Nwadike, ask me what question you can ask this spirit. Ask me so I can leave your house. I have been here too long," the dwarf shouted as it stopped pacing.

"Ahu Akunna, my ancestor, what question can I ask you? " my father said.

"Ask us Nwadike, 'If we do not know its father, do we know its mother?'" the dwarf Mask yelled and started to laugh, a dry, mirthless laughter. Then the Masks turned and left, screeching into the night.

That same night my father's youngest wife, pregnant and scared, was dragged away. I heard her cries. The night filled me with dread. A dread that remained even as I grew into adulthood, learnt the law, became a judge, and in time began to even see the night's events as a quasi-judicial charade.

I don't think I ever told you this, but wandering through our farms with two of my sisters many months later, I would see my father's discarded wife again, with a small child tied to her back. She told us she lived with a mechanic in the next village and had only come to to harvest the ede roots she had planted. She begged us not to tell anyone we had seen her.

Eucharia lifts the purple plastic bucket off her head and pours the hot water into the bath in one motion. We have been having problems with the water heater. Eucharia and I have had to improvise. When I settle into the tub, the water is hotter than I am used to. I don't mind. I immerse myself briefly, then lift my head out of the water and breathe.

I did visit your wife. Six months after you were buried. I took a bottle of port with me, wrapped in dark paper. Her eyes were bright. She seemed happy. She hugged me, draping her dark fleshy arms around my back. "He has gone. My Chike is gone," she said dramatically. I have always been uneasy around her.

"Sorry, so, so sorry. It must be such a shock," I said and hugged her again. We drank some of the port together. She insisted. Chike, our life together is everywhere. I straddled you -once- on the same divan on which your wife sits, sipping port from a wine glass.

The water is starting to cool. I can smell the plantains being fried in the kitchen. Our older daughter Ebuka will be visiting with her husband and children. Fried plantains are her children's favourite meal.

Our twins are grown now. Fully formed people living their own lives. I have stayed close to the moment of their conception, even as they have grown and moved inexorably from that point.

A year after we started, do you remember meeting me at the International Bar Conference in Barcelona? Do you remember the day after the conference ended when we sat at an outdoor café, drank coffee from small white porcelain cups, and rode the city bus to Basílica de la Sagrada Família? The sun was bright and strong, but it was a cool, pleasant day. You wore red shorts, and I wore a sundress, and we looked like tourists. I like thinking of that day.

An American couple on the bus kept looking at us. At the way I held on to you. "You guys look so sweet," the woman said.

"He's my husband," I said, smiling and looking up at you. I meant it then with all my heart.

"We know," said the man. "We can see your rings."

"Actually, I'm her lover," you said, laughter in your voice, "That's how I think of it."

"Aww. Aren't they so sweet," the woman said. "Kendrick and I have been married fifteen years, and he never tells me I'm his lover." And they both chortled knowingly.

The girls were conceived sometime during that trip.

It does not make sense, but I have always thought that the moment of their conception was on that bus. When I held on to you, looked at you, and gave you everything within me.

Eucharia knocks gently on the door. "Auntie Ebuka and her children are here," she says. I tell her to set the dining table and dish out the food. I will be out soon. I can hear our daughter's three children in the house. But I don't move to get out of the bath. I bury my head in the water. It is a while before I raise it again and breathe.

I found out I was pregnant on the same day my brother Okike died. It was death that occupied my mind. I could not think about the pregnancy.

I went back to Okija for the funeral. I left for the village a week before everyone, telling my husband it was to help with arrangements. Okike had built a grotesque mansion where our father's house had once stood, and I stayed in one of its empty rooms. You promised you would come. Each morning, as I eat a small breakfast in the empty dining room I hoped you would come that day. I had long conversations with myself that I imagined I would continue with you. In the quiet village air we would have space to talk and decide together what we would do.

In my dead brother's empty house, I wandered through the rooms, cleaning and dusting with the help of the caretaker's daughter, imagining so many possible futures. The days passed, but you didn't come.

Then the night before my brother's funeral, when the house was full of my siblings and their children, you sent me a message that you were in Okija. You asked me to meet you on the road that led from the market, at the outskirts of the village. "It would seem odd if I just drove to the house," you said.

When almost everyone had retired, I slipped downstairs and then, moving slowly, walked past the compound walls. It was a moonless night and the darkness closed in around me. I could feel my heart beat like a frenzied drummer within my chest. The shrieks of bats and cooing sounds of the owls frightened me. I walked on. As the darkness seemed to take form in front of me, in the shape of a thousand different terrors, I told myself that I was no longer a child that could be frightened by these inchoate fears of night. These admonishments did not stop my terror. I continued down the road in darkness because, like a child, I believed that you and joy lay at its end. Then I shrieked in horror. I thought I had seen an enormous snake with yellow malevolent eyes about to strike. It was nothing, a broken tail light and some bags twisted by my imagination into hideous form. I walked for fifteen minutes.

When I got to your car I was shaking. I told you nothing of my terror. We drove further away from the market to a clearing in the forest, where there was no road, and no one would see us. I was terrified of the night surrounding us, pressing against the car and the large tree leaves. We had sex in the car, with the oppressive, feral darkness around us. When we were finished, I told you I was pregnant. You were quiet, gentle and clear: "You should get an abortion," you said.

I lay with your scent, the taste of your mouth, and your fluids within me through the night. I cried until the sun started rising over Okike's house, and the cocks filled the air with their insistent crows. Then I rose and washed, put on the mourning uniforms my father's family had sown, and went to my brother's funeral. I didn't cry again.

There is a gentle knock on the door of the bathroom. It is our daughter Ebuka, she wants me to come out. She is checking if I'm ok. Her children want to see me. "I want to see you too, Mama."

I take a moment to catch my breath before I speak. "I will be right out," I say. I reach for a small towel and start to wash my face.

The Place at a Bend in The River

Things change. Sometimes they change for the worse. Sometimes, when I am in a melancholic mood, when Ngozi has gone for choir practice and I am alone in our flat, I think of how I have wasted my life. Perhaps, it is the same for everyone. In the end, shit comes down on all of us.

I have claimed the hours Ngozi spends at choir practice for myself. At fifty-six, I am at an age when I can look at life and admit that things are what they are. I've become exhausted with my efforts at lying to myself. I find I'm not yet tired of lying to others. I tell Ngozi I need to walk for my heart; it needs exercise. When she grabs her car keys and heads for choir practice, I wear a tracksuit and trainers. I know how I look. It is a ridiculous outfit. An overweight, over-indulged, middle-aged man acting out a pantomime of redemption. But this absurd uniform is my cover- the price I pay to leave the house every evening at seven thirty.

Ngozi claims it is unsafe to walk the streets of Lagos at night. Dressed as I am, I am a target. The cars! The drivers are so careless. If anything happened to you, I wouldn't know.

I find comfort in the streets. It's the noise that soothes me. The sound of human voices, muttering, coaxing, challenging, straining to be heard above the horns, the okadas, chirruping like birds…It reminds me of life around me, stubborn and gnarly, and my position floating above the fray. I am here by choice. The options my wife suggests are still open to me. My driver could drop me off at Ikoyi Club. Alternatively, if I insist on walking, he could take me to the safe gated streets of Banana Island, where many men and women like me form impromptu walking clubs.

Two times a week, I merely pretend to go walking. Instead, I go to visit Nidhi. She lives in a one-bedroom apartment along a dusty, untarred road. It is too far to walk, so I have an arrangement with an affable car-hire man. Oroki and I have settled into a routine. He waits for me at the foot of Falomo Bridge. I sit with him in front of the car. Somehow, I believe this makes it less likely that I will be caught. Oroki is always full of conversation. He leans back, his *fila* cocked at a jaunty angle. He is an

Ibadan man with deep long scarification lines across his cheeks.

Oroki and I have had this arrangement for about two years. Before they completed the Lekki Expressway, the trip could take hours. One evening, traffic was so bad that when I walked through Nidhi's door, she was already in her nightdress. I kissed her on the mouth and put one of her breasts in my mouth, biting at the thick, dark, fleshy nipple. But it was too late. I couldn't stay.

On the drive back to Victoria Island, I frantically searched for the lie I would tell Ngozi when I got home. I was still undecided when I opened the door of our flat. I worried for nothing. Ngozi had not stayed up. She was sleeping so soundly that I acted brave and took a shower.

Nidhi straddles me. Her hair falls over her shoulders, and I feel its ends on my upper thighs. She makes sharp, guttural noises as she rises and falls above me. When I am finished, she lays her breasts on my chest. Her hair falls on my face for a few seconds. Then she gets up, reaches to the nightstand, and grabs pieces of perforated tissue paper from a yellow cardboard box with two sharp tugs. In a practised motion, with the cupped tissue paper, she slides the used condom and its sack of yellow, dying sperm from my spent penis.

When she gets up to discard the tissue paper (and its contents) in the bathroom, I keep my eyes on her. Her body is beautiful. In ways her plain, pockmarked face cannot detract. A voluptuous body with large breasts so exquisitely shaped that it was disconcerting our first time. I felt I was looking at something I was not supposed to see.

When she returns to bed, she plays her hand down my back. I grab her hand and pull her down beside me. I don't tire of her body. Lying down, as she is now beside me, her stomach is flat without being gaunt or hard. When she stands, it protrudes slightly. A small scar runs below her belly button, like a small meandering river that suddenly bends towards her pubic hair. I wonder what upset left this rivulet on Nidhi's body. A childhood injury? Surgery? An appendectomy? An abortion? I don't ask. Instead, I trace my fingers along the river and let my finger skip to the place beneath. The hair is a wild forest tangled with undergrowth. A pungent, glistening, forested swamp. At first, this surprised me. I had become used to the modern convention of shaving, clipping and tending to every hair, even there.

Nidhi is a pharmacist. I met her at Shop-A-Lot, the large superstore where she works at the in-store pharmacy.

Kshitiz walked me down the aisle when I needed to refill my high blood pressure prescription. Kshitiz always walks too close to me, holding my elbow. It is a strange habit. My outfit provides him with accounting and audit services. On paper, we are a global operation, one of the world's largest accounting firms. In reality, we are a string of local fiefdoms cobbled together in loose partnership. The fiefdom in Nigeria is my outfit, mine until I retire when I turn sixty.

Kshitiz started with us modestly. He wanted our imprimatur, the name of our global firm, on his financial statements. He hid things from us; we only saw what he wanted us to see. Kshitiz only hired Indians in accounting and financial controls, twenty-four-year-old graduates straight from the Ahmedabad Institute of Management. When our eager cub accountants met with obfuscation or stonewalling from an Indian in accounting and raised a complaint to Kshitiz, the response was immediate. No problem! You will get the information! And an emphatic open gesture with the hand, like a firm wave. A wave that meant you would get nothing.

You see, Kshitiz inherited three stores from his father. He expanded cautiously- another room where things were going well, another floor built without shutting operations. In his forties, fifteen years after his father's death, he built another store. But something new is in the air. He has read about emerging African economies in *The Economist* and *Time Magazine*. Africa was rising. They were talking differently about the place where he had always lived.

Kshitiz also starts to think of himself in new ways. He no longer sees himself as a prosperous shopkeeper. Now, he has ambitions; he is a retailer, a pioneer, and a visionary. To help him complete the picture, he has started asking my outfit for management consulting services. Kshitiz spends modestly on these services - he is cautious, wary of being duped. Occasionally, he becomes effusive and free-spending. One afternoon he called me so persistently that I stepped out of a client meeting to take his call. What is Shop-A-Lot's expansion strategy? What are we doing about Distributed Distribution? These were phrases he had borrowed from someone. He used them tentatively, uncertain of what they might mean. I took advantage. I promised him a report and billed him.

My suggestion to pick up my medication at the in-store pharmacy pleased Kshitiz. He expressed mock outrage that I would buy anything anywhere else and then pointed out the clever way he had structured the in-house stores. A pharmacy, a bakery, and a phone shop. Each was an independent business owned by Indians whom he had been assured he could trust by a vast network of relatives. He charged them basic rent and a percentage of sales. It is very complicated, and it's straightforward, he said, pleased. It is not the type of thing that can work with Nigerians. Perhaps the look on my face causes him to think I am perplexed. "Africans don't understand retail business!" he exclaimed, laughing.

I don't find it surprising that he makes sweeping judgments so easily; categorisation is an old habit of the mind. He comes from a tradition that divides humanity into castes, each with its own traits. Certain attitudes have been baked into his skin. *It is a difference in civilisation.*

Kshitiz left me at the door of the in-house pharmacy. Perhaps as a concession to my medical privacy, he suggested we meet at his office when I was done.

Ngozi sits with me in the morning when I eat breakfast. She hardly eats anything. Breakfast- a feast in the morning- is not a meal that agrees with who she is. When we were still raising our girls, the noise and chatter at the breakfast table hid Ngozi's abstemiousness.

Now, when it is only Ngozi and me around the large dining room table, it is easy to observe the contrast. I stuff fried eggs and fried *akara* balls down my throat. Ngozi sits at the edge of her chair, picking at the toast on my side plate. Sometimes she smears a piece with jam before she puts it in her mouth.

Ngozi will be leaving soon for a meeting of her Lions Club charity. She is head of a committee raising money for Motherless Babies. After the girls left home, she started spending time on these church and charity affairs. Now, it is how she spends most of her time. It is not what I expected for her - this life, like my mother's.

Ngozi has always genuinely cared for others. This kindness is a quality that moves me and that has always drawn me closer to her. When the girls were still in secondary school, she came across an accident returning from a visit to her seamstress in Yaba. Traffic had slowed to a crawl, and everyone was driving past the older man bleeding at the side of the road. Ngozi stopped and picked him up. She then drove frantically to a hospital. The large nurse at the reception would not admit the man without a police report or an exorbitant deposit. Ngozi stayed with the man and persuaded the young doctor on duty to do what he could in the reception area. She went out to buy the medicine the young doctor needed. When she returned with the plastic bag containing gauze, antiseptic and antibiotics, she stayed. She watched the man die beside her in the waiting room. When Ngozi finally made it home- well past midnight- she cried, distraught, in my arms. He smelled so bad, she kept saying. It was probably all the blood turning rancid, but Ngozi said it smelled like death. I held and comforted her. But I also silently wondered how she could care so deeply for someone she did not even know.

Sometimes, I marvel at my wife, at her depth and variety. Ngozi, who can be so petty; Ngozi, who never forgives a wrong. It's this Ngozi who weeps for a stranger, as hard as she cried on hearing of the death of the father she adored.

I don't share Ngozi's religious faith. I am a sort of atheist. I orient myself in the world with my Igbo cosmology. I believe, and I don't believe. *Chi ne dum*, my *chi* guides me. When I let it. I know enough of the world to know it is the same with everyone else's god, even Ngozi's.

After Ngozi leaves, I gather my briefcase and files. I take my time. When I get to my car, I sit in the back. My driver, Gbenga, knows where to go. We make our way, through some traffic, to my office in Ikoyi. On the way, I don't read the newspapers Gbenga has placed folded on the seat beside me. I look out the window. On Sanusi Fafunwa Street, an attractive woman has stopped her Volkswagen Jetta in the middle of traffic. She jumps out of the car, screaming at the taxicab driver behind her. She is wearing tight-fitting jeans. She walks to the cab driver's window and points her finger in his face. The taxicab driver looks away, pretending to laugh. Even though she has stayed with me, in the end, I have disappointed Ngozi. She lets me cling to what I can. She averts her eyes. It is a kind of kindness.

As we pull into the office, the gatemen jump to attention. I am fond of the older one, Ibrahim. He used to be in the military. He never told me why he left.

Things change. A few months ago, the office was in flux. The heads of other fiefdoms –outfits in South Africa and London— saw the money we were making in Nigeria, and they wanted a piece. They suggested a committee to discuss a Single Africa Practice. They sent someone from London, one of the ambitious European partners. They expected him to ultimately head this Single Africa Practice. The sole reason for the proposed restructuring is to better serve our global clients, he told me in my office. I laughed out loud.

I knew the man they had sent from London. He was about my age. He had been born in Zimbabwe to British diplomats. I met him a few times at the Global Partners Retreat, and the Strategic Options Review Conference. He had tried to discuss Africa with me. I did not think he knew more than a bright child who reads newspapers. But he was full of conceit. "I have some thoughts,

Emeka. Something both of us can really dig into," he said, slapping my shoulder.

I won that fight. My fiefdom remained mine. On his side, all the man from London had was an idea. The idea that because men who looked like him had started this firm, it would always be controlled by men who looked like him. It is an idea born of a larger conceit.

While doing graduate work in London, midway through my first year, I had an argument with my thesis advisor. I was attempting to tell him that Western Europeans had successfully perpetrated the Great Theft. Every other human act of larceny or expropriation paled before it. Western European civilization, what he called Western Civilisation, had stolen everything. Every worthwhile idea that humans have ever had – will ever have – has been claimed by Western Civilization. Democracy? Yes, maybe the word, but the concept? How could the concept be yours? I asked, perplexed. How can physics belong to you? How can mathematics? One plus one is equal to two; is that yours as well? My advisor was polite, but he was confused. He hadn't understood what I meant.

Driven by this great conceit and his personal greed, this European had boarded a plane at Heathrow and flown here to steal from me. He expected he would be successful; Men who looked like him had done it before.

But other men create, adjust, and adapt. Sometimes, they are waiting for you when you get off the plane.

To celebrate a victory-an exclusive distributorship, an agency arrangement – Kshitiz organises dinner parties at the large Chinese restaurant off Kingsway Road. It is a large complex on three floors. Kshitiz reserves a large private room on the top floor, away from the other diners. The private room is supposed to be impressive, with plush red carpets and wood panelling with gold accents, but in it, I feel shabby.

Kshitiz organised this dinner to celebrate the Private Equity Investment executives discussing putting money into his business. I know the organisation. At the top is a rock musician who was once famous for organising concerts that raised money for famine relief in Africa. Now, he has branched out. He has convinced men with money in London, Dubai and Tokyo to give some to him. He will triple the money investing in the New Africa. I know how it sounds. It is ridiculous. But the entire thing does not appear strange to anyone else. They have been given millions. Kshitiz is here to get some of it.

It is a family affair. Along with his key executives, Kshitiz has invited his son and daughter. I have never met Kshitiz's wife.

I like Kshitiz's son. He is quiet and polite. He understands he is out of his depth. He observes his father. He wants to understand how he can keep what will come to him. There is anxiety about him. It is the listlessness of a simple, settled man who can feel things changing.

While we wait for the money men, the conversation is about Kshitiz's son's wedding. The bride will be in Lagos in a fortnight from Mumbai. It will be her first visit to Nigeria. As a concession to modern times, Kshitiz explains, he has agreed for her to make this trip. She will stay for a week, and then everyone will fly to India for the wedding. Her father is very prominent, very influential, Kshitiz confides conspiratorially.

I have travelled with Kshitiz. I have seen him at the airport. When the queue on the visitors' line is long, he makes a big show of using his Nigerian passport. He speaks to those in the Nigerians line, helpfully pointing him to the visitors' desk. But I am a Nigerian. I was born here. My children were born here. He brandishes the green passport above his head. People in the queue laugh or smile. Some make a point of coming over to shake his hand. My brother, one says.

It occurs to me that Kshitiz might once have been as unsettled as his son. That he might once have felt the same anxiety. Washed up, as it were, on some foreign shore. Committed to surviving and thriving, but not to belonging.

When the money men arrive, Kshitiz's daughter springs up to greet them. She is effusive, kissing them on the cheeks. For the first time, I reflect on how close she is in height to Nidhi. Kshitiz's daughter has a thinner build. They must both be about the same age, the same age as my older daughter.

I sense Kshitiz's discomfort. He bought his daughter a flat in London. She spent a few years there studying for a diploma in interior design. Now she is back in Lagos, she organises art exhibitions showing young contemporary Nigerian artists. She spoke to me about my outfit sponsoring one of her shows. I wasn't happy about her request. But it had to be assented to. I wrote out an adequate cheque.

It is all this art business that concerns Kshitiz. She is out late with these Nigerian artists. He sees her hugging them at the shows. Kshitiz is worried about what else could be going on.

The evening went well. The money men are reassured. Kshitiz's daughter has offered to show the former rock star the most promising new artists. He wants something new to add to his collection.

We spent a long time in the parking lot saying goodnight. Each handshake is followed by a hug. The rock star, the other money men in their tailored suits, Kshitiz, Kshitiz's Indian managers, everyone gets in on it. Even the Mobile Police officer who provides security to Kshitiz's daughter seems pleased. He holds the door for her with a big smile on his face. Then the convoy of black SUVs with bright xenon lights departs into the night.

I am the last to leave. Gbenga drives me home. I look out at the street and traffic, even this late into the night. It is too late to go walking.

When we were in university, and I was chasing her, I would tell Ngozi stories about my uncle Odukwe. When I was a child, he had chosen me as his *oko akpa*. Ngozi had not known what that meant. You Township people don't know anything, I had said. She had rocked back on the thin, iron frame bed and laughed. Ok, Village Boy, what does it mean?

An *oko akpa* is the child that carries an elder's bag and stool to meetings. When I was a child, in my village, it was a privileged position. You got to hear men speak to other men.

At dinner, one of the money men had told a story. Something that had happened to him at the airport, coming in. A customs officer had engaged him in conversation. The officer had seemed intrigued with the

149

concept of Private Equity Investment – that the money man was in Lagos to invest in other people's businesses. What kinds of business? he wanted to know. The money man explained that they looked at various sectors but were keen on consumer businesses. So if I show you a good business for consumers, you will invest? the customs officer asked. At that point, the money man laughed and told the customs officer that the minimum investment amount was ten million United States dollars. At that point, the conversation turned nasty. The customs officer became aggressive. In that case, what did you bring for us? he asked, tapping on his desk. How can you say nothing? You just used your smelly mouth to tell me your minimum investment is ten million dollars.

Kshitiz had told the money man the customs officer only wanted money. Five or ten dollars would have settled it. I said nothing. When I got into the car, I remembered my uncle Odukwe had retired as a customs officer.

My village is in Ozubulu, about fifteen miles from Onitsha if you go through the road to Nnewi.

Last Christmas, my daughters came home. It's been unusual these past few years for all four of us to be together at home. The girls are the part of my life that has, miraculously, remained clear, unmixed with mud.

They have learnt to see the world clearly, with their own eyes.

The day after Christmas, we had people over for a long lunch. I had the bitter-leaf soup. The meal was exquisite.

After lunch, speaking with the Swiss Ambassador, I was boasting that no Nigerian president has ever worn a suit and tie, nor any Western clothing on state business, right from independence.

I spoke with pride, comparing this small part of our country's history with that of other African countries. All with leaders in smart Western suits that unintentionally betrayed how little had changed.

The Swiss Ambassador is an old bachelor with whom I occasionally play chess. He looked at me with a small smile, then said that sartorial purity was little compensation for everything Nigeria's leaders had put the country through. I started arguing forcefully. I wanted an acknowledgement from him of what I had meant. But I was floundering. I feared his observation, which I considered obvious and trite, would detract from the pleasure I had taken in the afternoon.

It was my older daughter, Ada, who had saved the moment for me. Daddy, that's only true if you don't count military uniforms. Those uniforms are suits, aren't they? They're certainly Western.

Indeed, they are, the Swiss Ambassador conceded. I jumped in as if Ada had supported the argument I had been making. Ada, you are quite right. It's those uniforms and what they represent that did us in.

I knew what to do with the argument from that point. I was on familiar ground. I could go at the Swiss Ambassador for a few more minutes, but I was tired of this game. I wanted to find out what my twenty-four-year-old daughter might have to tell me. I walked with her to the patio, where dusk was settling on Lagos, our city.

The length of my relationship with Nidhi has surprised me. I have had these arrangements with women before. I am generous with gifts, and money. Sometimes I pay the rent, or for phones, or medical bills for relatives. I understand what I have to offer, and I am willing to trade.

Nidhi's demands are modest. Occasionally, she has surprised me with a large request, but these have been tentative and quickly withdrawn.

Lately, she has been hinting at a desire to leave Nigeria. Not to go back to India but to the United States for graduate education. All her family is here in Nigeria. She was born here. Her older sister, for years her roommate, got married to a man from Gujarat.

Nidhi says her father pesters her. The man calls her twice a week from Onitsha, where he lives. He once had a thriving business importing cheaply manufactured shoes and clothes from India and Bangladesh. The business collapsed. Now, his shirts and blouses compete with second-hand clothing imported in bales by Igbo traders. He wants Nidhi to get married, like her sister. He wants her to move in with relatives in Idumota. The same relatives that own the in-store pharmacy.

Nidhi is playing with the idea of a different life. She is talking about a Masters in Business Administration in the United States. I had not taken her up on her hints. I was afraid it would cost me enough money to produce entanglements. But now, in this scheme, I also see a way to bring this to an end.

So, while she plays with the hairs on my chest, occasionally rubbing my round, protruding belly, I ask her what she has in mind. She wants me to sponsor her Masters in America. She speaks insistently, clear-eyed. I'm surprised by the abruptness and the desperation, and the bigness of her request.

What kind of MBA? What type of school? Is she thinking of the Ivy League? An executive MBA program? Does she want a focus on finance or marketing? What kind of job does she have in mind after graduation? Jobs in America, she says. This is as far as she has gone. This is as far as she has thought it through.

I am weary. I have wasted my life. I raise myself up. I reach for her hair, slip my fingers in it, and slide them through. I lay her on her back. I put my penis into her mouth. She sucks at it. I can feel a release building up from beneath me. I pull out of her mouth and watch the thick globs of translucent semen settle on her lips and chin.

Nidhi is looking at me. There is no resentment on her face. This is what she expected.

In the Convalescent Ward

My husband was in my mouth, still erect, when I heard him snoring.

When the storm started, I was curled in a ball, my back arched in rage, lying in bed beside Ogene. Against my will, it seemed, my hands trembled. I couldn't cry. Ogene snored gently, the sound of his moist breath drowned by the intensifying slap and patter of rain, slashed by the wind against our roof and windows. My phone, balanced precariously on the nightstand, began to vibrate, shifting with a steady pulsating motion till it fell. I picked it off the floor and answered. It was the Matron.

Mercifully, she was calling me in to complete Nneka's shift.

I get dressed noisily, knocking things about as I put on my uniform. Ogene sleeps through it. Only when I snap the dresser close does he wake, startled. He stares at me with wide, unblinking eyes, like a student struggling for comprehension.

"Where are you going?" he growls.

"Where does it look like I am going?" I reply.

He continues to stare at me, and then, as if he has suddenly seen enough, he turns around on the bed, hugs his pillow and goes back to sleep.

It was one of those night storms that came with the rains in Owerri, bursting upon the town's red soil and stretches of thin, black asphalt with sustained, mean violence. In the morning, sitting in the staff room drinking tea, I would read in the newspaper that a lorry driver, blinded by sheets of rain, had driven his truck and its load of Thai rice into the Catholic Cathedral.

I got drenched walking from my car to the reception hall. Dirty puddle water sloshes out of my shoes. I can't tell if I am crying. The rain falls on my head and runs down my face, and the pain in my eyes and the bridge of my nose feels the same either way. I pull at the front of my uniform, separating its wetness from my body. Then I wipe the rain from my face with the palm of my hand and walk into the ward.

It is almost empty. There are fourteen metal frame beds arranged in two rows. A few with white mosquito nets hung above them like shrouds. The air is thick with the sweet smell of sickness and disinfectant.

Someone has opened a few of the wooden window shutters, and gusts of air blow in from the dying storm.

Above the closing whistles of the wind, I can hear the murmurs of low voices, laboured breathing, and an occasional low, racking cough. From the far corner of the ward comes the distinct grating sound of metal scraping. At the head of the ward, in the almost darkness, a pool of light falls from a large yellow light bulb on the nurses' station. I turn to it.

"Nurse, nurse! Please come. Biko," a man calls. I turn around and walk to the sound. The man is bent over, scraping sardines from a tin can with a spoon, trying to feed a grey-haired woman propped up on a thin pillow. The woman murmurs, her eyes closed. Sweat has seeped through her thin chemise and formed dark blotches on her chest and left side. "Biko, nurse, she is not eating. She has been like this since afternoon." The man draws out his thin arm, the skin drooping from it like a shallow inverted mound, opens the palm of his hand and gestures to the woman.

I take her pulse, using the watch pinned to my uniform. Then I pick up the chart clipped to the bed and read a little. There is no hope now. She will be gone soon. The cancer surgery wasn't recommended. It was pointless, but someone had insisted and was ready to pay. "She will be ok," I say "just let her rest." I touch him high on his shoulders as I turn towards the nurse's station. "Grandpa, you too should rest. You don't want to also get sick." His head drops and he starts to unfurl a raffia mat on the concrete floor beside the bed. "Dalu, thank you, my daughter," he calls after me and starts coughing.

As I approach the nurses' station, I see Matron and the two other nurses on duty sitting in a semi-circle on black rolling chairs around the nurses' desk. A fourth chair, with a missing arm, is set apart. "Nneka started vomiting again. I decided she should go home," Matron says as I get close. She is wearing a dark grey cardigan, over her white uniform.

"That's unusual this late in pregnancy," Nurse Adanma says, "but she will be ok." Nurse Adanma has six children. She lets everyone know she has had seven pregnancies.

"Nneka's pregnancy has really been unusual. It's often like that the first time." Nurse Obioma adds. Nurse Obioma is the mother of three.

They all seem to turn to me as if they want to hear what I have to add. I don't say a word. I pull out the ward file and, still standing, start to flip through the pages.

"Sorry for dragging you from your husband in this bad weather," Matron says, smiling and placing a hand on my waist. I take a deep breath. And the image of Ogene hugging a pillow, slips into my head. I let it linger for a moment before I turn and smile at the Matron.

"At least your husband doesn't have to worry about getting children ready for school by himself in the morning," Nurse Adanma says. "Anytime I am on night shift, my husband abuses me the entire week."

"It is still difficult leaving your husband in the middle of the night for shift," Nurse Obioma says in a conciliatory tone.

I pause in the notes and turn to Nurse Adanma, "You didn't do your 1 a.m. ward round," I say. She turns to me. Her eyes are hard. Then she laughs, "I did it o! Nurse prefect!"

"It is not in the file," I say.

"I haven't written it," she snaps back. "I haven't had time. I waited with Nneka for her husband. Biko, don't carry your frustration to me."

"What frustration?" I ask.

"If you don't know, it's not me that will tell you," she answers.

"Just do your job Adanma," I say.

"Calm down, both of you," Matron says. "Adanma, go and do the round." Matron pulls a small green and white tube of Vicks Inhaler and places it in her nostril.

"This rainy weather always disturbs me," she says to no one in particular after she inhales.

Nurse Adanma gets up and lifts the dark grey, cast-metal encased sphygmomanometer sitting on the desk. I sit down in the vacated chair as soon as she stands. She turns back to look at me, hisses, and then continues to do her round.

"Let me come and help you," Nurse Obioma says, getting up to join her.

The Matron puts a placating hand on my thigh. "Ndidi, patience, patience," she murmurs. "Mtcheeew," I exclaim, puckering my lips and sucking in the air.

Later that morning, at the end of my shift, I would stop at the far end of the ward to look in on the old woman and the old man. She would be breathing easier, and her eyes would be open. The old man would grasp my hand and thank me. "She is my one and only wife," he would say to me, a wonderful smile on his face. "She can't die. Not before I die." He would introduce me to his wife, and she would smile weakly and then close her eyes.

I am jolted awake by the loud banging on our front door.

When I come to the door it is my husband's sister. She is sweating and mopping her forehead with a purple hand towel. "I thought you may be sleeping," she says, as she pushes her large body through the front door. "Ogene said you did the night shift." She is dressed in a purple, lace, up-and-down, with a matching head wrap. In her right hand is a black plastic bag.

"We had a function," she says. "I brought you some food." She hands the plastic bag to me and settles herself on the brown couch in the sitting room, sighing as her weight comes off her feet. I glance into the black plastic bag and walk to the kitchen. "Will you drink water?" I ask, before I pass through the door.

She drinks the water greedily, both hands wrapped around the tall glass. When she finishes, she smacks her lips, making a wet slapping sound. As I take the glass from her hand, she clears her throat.

She is an Apostle at the Christ Mission Evangelical Church and had insisted that her pastor officiate our wedding. It wasn't what I wanted. I was younger then, unsure how to resist. Ogene had insisted. "No way! If you leave her, she will want her church in everything we do." We were married in the Catholic Cathedral, just as I wanted.

"Let me ask you, Ndidi, what is the problem that you are not telling me?"

"What do you mean?" I ask, pretending I don't know what she is alluding to.

"Ogene won't tell me anything. But it has been five years! What is the problem?" She shifts her weight on the couch and pats the space beside her. Her face is set in a half-smile. "It is when you discuss a problem that you get a solution," she adds. "Please sit down, Ndidi"

I am standing over her with the empty glass in my hand. "Let me drop this in the kitchen."

"No need. Just leave it on the table," she says.

I am tired and angry. And I need to sleep. She stays another hour.

"I will take you. Just come! Our pastor is a miracle worker. We have a function for this kind of problem. I will take you to him myself. Nothing is too big for Jesus!" she says as she reluctantly moves through the front door.

I am exhausted. If she had taken any of my many hints and left, even a minute ago, this would have been a cordial visit. But now I can feel the rage held down in my throat being poked by her grating voice. I look at her round, sweating face.

"Take your brother to your pastor," I say. "Akwa, nothing is beyond Jesus."

"You insolent girl," she exclaims, turning to me, "Mind yourself." But it is too late. She has crossed the threshold. I close the door in her face. "Mtcheeew!" she exclaims, from the other side of the door. "I don't blame you," she shouts "it is my brother I blame." I hear her feet shuffling down the stairs.

I draw the curtains tight, so they shield against the strong noon sun, and lay down in the muted orange glow that filters through the fabric and falls on our bed. I lay awake for a while. My mind is restless. I call Ogene. It rings, but he does not pick up. It is the middle of the day, and it is a busy time at the bank I tell myself as I put the phone aside. I turn off the ringer so I will not be awakened if it rings, but also so, free from knowing whether Ogene has bothered to call back, I can fall asleep.

The twilight would disorient me, and when I woke from my nap, I would think I had slept through to morning. As I sat up in bed, I would look out the window to an empty space in the small car park of our tenement apartment and realise that Ogene had still not come home. I would pick up my phone and see he hadn't called. There would be a text saying he was busy in the office. I would have forty-five minutes before my shift would start.

I stand on the concrete veranda outside the ward with my phone against my ear. It is dark, and the lights which should light up the veranda are all out. The rain drizzles softly, but makes a sharp, echoing noise on the tin roof.

My brother is laughing on the line. "Take it easy," he says. "Don't mind her. I know she went to look for trouble. Ogene is a good man."

"Mtcheeew," I respond.

"Nmba, don't do that," my brother says. "That's not fair. Ogene is solid."

"Whose side are you on, sef?" I ask.

"You know I am always on your side. But you know how you are sometimes. You need to take things easy. What has he done?" he says.

"He should be defending me from this nonsense!" I say. "How can he allow his sister to come to our house to talk to me like that?"

"But he didn't send her," my brother says.

"She is his sister. He is the one that gives her space. Even if he didn't send her, he sent her," I say. My brother laughs.

"You know he didn't send her. She is crazy in her own way," he adds after he stops.

I see Nurse Adanma poke her head through the ward door and then turn and glare at me. I stare back at her. "It is fifteen minutes to your ward round," she says and smiles as if she is just being helpful.

"Hold on," I say loudly to my brother so Adanma can hear, "there is a jobless person here eavesdropping on our conversation." And start to walk further down the veranda.

"Mtcheeew!" Adanma turns back into the ward.

I was pregnant at our wedding. Ogene had insisted. "It is proof of compatibility," he said and laughed, leaning in to wrap his arms around me on my dorm bed. "So, you won't marry me if I can't have a baby?" I had asked, laughing a small, tentative laugh as I settled against his chest.

"You know I love you. We are just making sure," he said and smiled a wonderful smile. There was kindness in his eyes. And I knew he was just being reasonable.

"How is your application for America going?" my brother asks. "When you get there and start making American nurse money, you people shouldn't forget us o."

"The application is moving. I have taken the qualification exam. The agency says it will be less than nine months now. Ogene disturbs me about it all the time. He is the one who makes sure that all the documents are being filed on time. Once I get my visa, he can get his too. He is tired of Nigeria."

"Who is not tired?" my brother says.

During my round, I stop at the old woman's bed. The old man is still there. She seems to be getting better. She is sitting up on the bed, and he is spooning rice and a red stew out of a plastic bowl into her mouth. Her right hand trembles. I notice the old man's clothes have not changed. "Didn't you go home?" I ask.

"No, my daughter. Since they finished the surgery, I have been here with her. Sometimes, when she is sleeping well, I go to the back of the hospital and ease myself. The boys there bring me water to wash," he says. I stay and talk to him for some time. His wife is weak and doesn't speak. She smiles when the son in America who paid for the surgery is mentioned. Another son comes in the evening with food and provisions. "She is getting stronger," the old man beams at me. "Do you think we will be leaving soon?" he asks, and even though the smile is still on his face, I see the sad doubt, thick around the rims of his eyes. I nod my head. "God willing," I say.

It was those bewildered eyes you see in the lovers of the sick, eyes that see death is coming long before their minds comprehend it. In a future, then still far away, at the Sweetwater Hospital in Monroe, Tennessee, I would see the same eyes on women with white, dry skin and brown blotches as they looked at old men with oxygen masks fitted firmly over pale noses and dry mouths.

My husband is pulling away from me, his hips starting to spread as he rolls off my body and onto his side. I hold the back of his head, and he stops. He looks at me and smiles. I feel myself smiling weakly. He kisses my forehead, then continues his roll till he is on his back staring at the ceiling. There is silence between us. Then, like someone who suddenly remembers food forgotten on a hot stove, he sits up. "Have you completed the agency experience affidavits? Do you have all the signatures?" he asks. "I will try and send them by DHL in the morning. Latest by Friday," he adds.

"Is that what you are thinking about now?" I ask.

"We have to get it in as soon as possible. I spoke to Ann at the agency. With your scores, she is sure you will get a sponsor."

"I want us to go and see a doctor. They have a package at Egwu Fertility," I say.

"Why are you even thinking of that nonsense. When we get to America, we can go to a correct clinic. If there is even any need."

"It has been five years."

"Five years," he repeats quietly. "Don't be surprised once we enter America, you will fall pregnant," and starts laughing, as if it was a good joke.

I lift myself from the bed and cover my body with a wrapper. When I leave the bedroom, Ogene is still in bed, gazing at the ceiling. I boil some water to make tea. Then, with the mug warming my fingers, I sit on the brown couch and look through the windows. Soon I hear Ogene start to snore through the half-open bedroom door.

It was one of those nights that we had in our small

flat in Owerri, during the raining season. When I was happy for a roof under which I could sit and watch the unending rain beating down on the red land and the poor lonesome figures caught in the storm. They were always moving, sprinting in the downpour, trying to take cover under flimsy sheds, and then giving up entirely, walking through the thin streets with the lowered shoulders of people who had now suffered the worst, who no longer cared.

In the morning, before the first ward round, I would mark a time of death for the old woman. The old man, still bewildered, would hold on to my hand with both of his, as if he wished to stop something that had already happened. He would trudge, shuffling his feet, behind the orderlies that carried her body away. "My daughter, where are they taking my wife?" he would turn to ask me. And I would wrap my arms around his shoulders, and he would cry, his mouth open and his lips quivering. Later that afternoon, during my break, in the staff room, I would start to fill out my supporting application for an immigrant visa to America. On the form, where it sought my marital status, in blue ink, I would tick the box marked "Divorced (No Dependents)."

We Told Wonderful Lies

They dance a daring, synchronised dance, flying up through the air and dropping to the earth and the body, each racing the other. The two blue-bellied flies, in their persistence, seem to be mocking the solemnity of the mourners that shuffle past the open casket. A reminder that a human corpse is rotting flesh, he thinks, as he reaches the foot of the coffin.

He cannot keep his face in the compact of sustained, mournful gravitas. Men and women, all in black clothing, fill the pews on either side. Before him, a line of black-clothed mourners winds like a slack lasso around the white, gold-handled casket. He turns his face to the ground. Tufts of yellow-green crabgrass bloom in the cracks on the cement floor. A short column of black ants marches to an unknown destination. He lifts his eyes and looks into the casket.

Maximum's body lies still - fixed, dead. What holds

his gaze is Maximum's flesh, now a greenish copper with the light reflecting off it in a metallic sheen. He relaxes the muscles of his face, so his expression is serious and vacant.

At the head of the corpse, he shuffles past the high-backed chairs placed before the first pews, as if for visiting dignitaries. Maximum's family are seated in the high-backed chairs. Some mourners veer off to offer the family hugs, hand grasps, or solemn, sympathetic nods. The hugs are administered awkwardly, with the consolers standing and the family seated. Maximum's mother sits at the end of the row. She has a black scarf around her head and wears no makeup. Her eyes are open, dry and vacant. Wisps of grey hair slip from beneath her scarf.

Other mourners - those that don't feel entitled to dramatic demonstrations of grief before the bereft-shuffle off to the back of the church. He takes this path. As he slips past, he sees Killer, Chinwendu, and Puff-Puff have approached the high-back chairs. Killer has Maximum's mother in an embrace so purposeful that she has risen and started to wail in Killer's arms. He cannot tell from where he stands if tears have come to her eyes.

It is getting dark. The empty beer bottles on the square wooden table attract flies. The flies make lazy short hops on the table top. He watches them impassively. When one of the flies mounts another and then a third begins to clamber on top he feels a sudden, sharp disgust.

With nightfall, the green bottles have turned a dark purple. The air is still infused with the odour of fresh and stale alcohol. "You people should come and collect these bottles now!" The broad wave of Killer's arm disturbs the flies. They fly off but quickly return. "Where that small girl? Bia, bring three more Star. And two more pepper soup. Puff-Puff, you still dey chop?" Killer's voice is wavy, smoothed with alcohol.

Puff-Puff drops his spoon. He lifts the ceramic bowl to his lips, tilts his head, and drains what remains of his pepper soup. His round, cherubic face glistens with sweat. One could mistake Puff-Puff for a happy, overweight adolescent schoolboy.

"Abeg, add one more pepper soup," Puff-Puff says. Killer waves the serving girl off and leans his weight against the back of the plastic chair.

The night settles like dark sediment around them. He knew they would all meet here tonight. This is the place where they come to drink. He has slipped off his shoes and can feel his soles against the smooth plastered cement.

They are quiet for a while. He listens to the buzz of the tubes of fluorescent light. Killer speaks first. "So this is how Maximum's life finished. Gone, just like that," Maximum is dead, it is natural Killer should believe himself the new leader, he thinks.

Chinwendu mutters, "I can't believe it."

"The man is dead," Puff-Puff says, shaking his head "what can't you believe?"

Fresh bottles of Star soon appear. The serving girl lingers, opening each bottle at the table. Killer lifts his bottle. "To Maximum!" he says, and the others at the table raise their glasses.

"Ah! But you people lied today, o! Kai!" Puff-Puff chortles, "Na Cicero own wey wan' kill me pass: 'He was a good man, a gentle colossus, showing kindness to his fellow men.'" Puff-Puff laughs wildly, slamming his palm on the wooden table and sending panicked flies flying off. "Cicero! Where you learn English like that? Even me, myself, I wan' begin cry."

He had given a funeral oration. After Killer and Chinwendu spoke, he climbed the pulpit and gave a speech. He had taken quite some time thinking about what he would say. For some reason it had seemed important to him that the speech be one Maximum would like. A eulogy that was elegant, simultaneously telling truth and lie. He looks up at Puff-Puff and smiles. "Wetin you wan' make I talk? It's a funeral. We are required to tell lies. We told wonderful lies."

He speaks quietly, in a tone he modulates to be friendly. He has started to tire. He wants only to stay as long as he needs to without giving offence. He makes an effort to laugh whenever Puff-Puff tells a joke. He looks around. There are no other customers. They are together without distractions. His phone starts to buzz. He digs it out of the front pocket of his jeans and lays it on the table. He can see it is his girlfriend, Nnemka. The phone continues buzzing. Everyone at the table ignores it. It stops. Then it starts again.

"Ol' boy, answer am now! Na your wife?" Chinwendu says.

He picks up the phone and puts it back in his pocket. He can feel it there, continuing to vibrate. "Stop calling that girl my wife," he says to Chinwendu.

Puff-Puff chuckles, "Na your wife now."

He thinks of the start of his morning. He had cupped one of Nnemka's small breasts with his left hand and pulled himself on top of her. She heaved under him. When a deep, un-relinquished moan escaped from inside him, he had looked at Nnemka's dark, beautiful face, with the light brown wisps of hair that reached past the side of her ear and felt his body flood with relief and joy, exultant.

The moment hadn't lasted. He felt the slow, jerky, ruinous convulsion, her hand on his shoulder, her voice strange, like a Nollywood film actor's, shouting: "I'm coming, I'm coming." And he, defeated, felt his weight fall through her and into the mattress, his body heavy with resentment because he knew she had been faking an orgasm. He rolled off her and sat quietly at the edge of the bed. "Baby, what's wrong?" she had asked.

He can still feel the phone buzzing in his trousers. He gets up, pulls it out, puts it to his ear, says "Hello," and starts to walk away from the table.

"Woman wrapper," Killer calls after him. Puff-Puff and Chinwendu laugh.

"Pussy whipped," Puff-Puff shouts. There is more laughter.

He watches his mother, a small dark woman with flecks of grey hair, walk out of the kitchen with a large white bowl filled with egusi soup. "Maximum, you will enjoy this soup. Uju, remove that book from there."

His sister takes her large, grey intermediate chemistry textbook off the dining room table.

"Auntie, you know I always enjoy your soup. I am always hinting Cicero that we should come and visit, but he pretends he doesn't understand," Maximum says, smiling an open, pleading smile.

His mother's laughter is loud, her mouth open so he

can see her well-spaced teeth. "You people should stay on campus and read, not come here to eat soup."

Uju, in her pink and blue school uniform, turns in her chair, so she faces Maximum. "I don't know why you are attending university here in Enugu. Me, I'm going to University of Lagos."

"Finish secondary school first," Maximum says, laughing.

"Don't mind her," his mother says, scooping a big mound of eba and the rich, yellow-grained soup onto a large serving plate in front of Maximum.

He is thirsty. He pushes the chair back, rises from the table and walks to the tall refrigerator in the far corner of the dining room. He notices that the refrigerator door handle is worn and its false wood veneer peeled. Inside, the fridge smells musty, as if it's failing in some way. He opens a bottle of water and pushes it to his lips.

"Ukaonu, bring another bottle of water for Maximum and come and sit down and eat," his mother says, before turning to his sister. " You, have you washed your hands?" Uju gets up to wash her hands.

After lunch, his mother called him into her room. He tapped twice on the dark grey plywood door. His mother was seated on the bed, a small square of Naira notes neatly folded in her hands. "Ukaonu, sit down," she patted a spot beside her on the thin brown blanket.

It was this way between them, he thought, this intimacy, like her life, was tethered to his fate. It was an intimacy he could not separate from memories of his dead father, from his mother's need for both a dutiful son and ceremonial head of household.

"Why do your friends call you Cicero? Do you know even that nickname makes me happy? Do you know why?"

He thought the questions, the topic, odd. As he had grown older he had become used to the set ways in which he and his mother spoke. The topics and the themes ritually touched upon. He anticipated that the question was a new prelude to some admonition or praise. He expected it would end with a moral lesson.

He was always deferential when he spoke to his mother. The sacrifice she had made - was still making - to educate him and his sisters sat, like a corpulent market woman, on his conscience. Her primary school teacher's salary was supplemented by work as a seamstress, raising chickens, and selling eggs, biscuits, and sardines in tins. The memory of her standing over him as he did practise maths questions for the university entrance exams - correcting, nagging, supporting. Politely, he answered her. Told her that he didn't know why she liked that his nickname was Cicero.

He waited for the lesson, almost sharing vicariously

in the joy he imagined his mother would feel in unravelling it. Another block, perhaps even decorative, supplementing the edges of a well-laid foundation. He wanted her to be happy. It was his fondest desire.

"Because Cicero is a scholar. And even when they are joking, your friends know that you are a serious student. It makes me happy." She squeezed the fold of notes into his hand. "It is only four hundred, but they will pay us soon." His hand closed around the notes. "Mummy, thank you," he said.

In his second year, when he was back on break from university, he had driven her to school on a late Friday evening to pick up her promised salary. She had come back into the car with a folded newspaper. "Look!" she shouted, thrusting the newspaper at him. He had thought it was an article explaining again why teachers' salaries hadn't been paid, but it wasn't. It was a story about violent fraternities in universities. The article was filled with lurid, ridiculous stories. She hissed. "How can children raised by human beings behave like…." Before she finished, he had started laughing. She had looked at him puzzled, for a moment. "What is funny?" she asked.

"The way you said 'Children raised by human beings'." He started laughing again. She smiled a bit, and then she laughed too.

When they left, his mother, a worn red-spotted,

yellow, wax-print wrapper around her waist, hugged him to her chest. This always touched him. "My son, jisike. Keep it up. One year to graduation." Then he and Maximum closed the doors of the old Toyota Cressida and drove off, his mother and sisters waving at them as they passed through the gates. His mother waved with both arms above her head.

On the short drive back to campus, they stopped by a roadside kiosk so Maximum could buy cigarettes. The street was quiet. Three uncompleted houses, with their unfinished facades of grey concrete blocks, gave the road the desolate air of a wrecked, abandoned place.

Maximum jumped over the open drainage ditch between the road and the kiosk and paid for five sticks of Marlboro. The old man in the kiosk put the cigarette sticks in a discarded Benson & Hedges pack.

He leaned against the bonnet of the old Cressida and scanned the low horizon with his eyes. Maximum lay on the bonnet, his feet were planted on the car's hood, his legs bent at the knee. They drew smoke into their lungs. After a few minutes passed, they talked in low voices. Maximum's voice was sure, deep, and almost tender. "This life is starting to be sweet. In less than one year, I will be in law school in Lagos," Maximum said, as his eyes shone.

He looked across at Maximum, took another drag of the cigarette, and crushed the glowing, shrivelling butt beneath his boot.

Maximum drove. The Cressida moved smoothly, music blasting from a new Pioneer CD player fitted in the dusty, brown plastic dashboard.

"Abeg put the slow jams CD," Puff-Puff said. "Chinwendu, wetin dey do you?! See it there!" Chinwendu leaned forward in the front passenger seat and slipped the CD burnt with a DJ's selection of slow R&B music into the player.

"Na wa for you and that CD," Killer said.

"The music dey cool my head when we dey go mission," Puff-Puff said, closing his eyes.

Puff-Puff was in the back of the car, sandwiched between him and Killer. This was the second time he was going to the university at Okigwe. The first had been for a party. They were almost there. He wound down his window to let in the night air.

They had agreed upon a meeting point under a tree just after the rusty car left the four-lane expressway. Four Vice Admirals were standing, waiting. He noticed one of them was smoking and that he tapped the ash from his cigarette by flipping his thumb against the cigarette's butt. In the darkness, the cigarette's glow and the old Toyota's dim headlights were the only light.

He watched as Maximum opened his door and stepped out. Killer followed. In the dim light, they held out their right arms to the four men and exchanged the Vice Lord salute. Then, in a semicircle, they bent their heads in conference. He noticed flying insects, termites probably, starting to swirl in the pool of the weak headlights.

"Cicero, I beg come," Maximum called, turning back to him in the car. He opened the car door and put his feet in the red, dusty dirt. Sweat stuck his shirt to his back.

"This is the guy. And this is his roommate. Room 22 Akanu Ibiam Hall. They are both Axes," the man with the cigarette said, handing him two photographs and a folded piece of paper.

"Complete elimination?" Maximum asked.

The smoker smiled a lascivious, almost lewd smile. "Complete," the smoker replied.

They entered the squalid university dorm room just before 2 a.m. Surprisingly, the door was unlocked, and the fluorescent lights were on. Maximum, tall and muscular, stood guard at the head of the stairs. Puff-Puff, standing at the door, craned his neck to see. He struck first, bringing the butcher's knife down into the sleeping roommate on the top bunk. Chinwendu's blow came next and then he stabbed again; the sleeping man had hardly started to shout before he was quiet again. He didn't see the man's face. He only saw a threadbare grey blanket that looked like it had been lightly dabbed with blood.

The man in the bottom bunk had not stirred. Undisturbed, supine, with a plain face which appeared so open, innocent and free of sin. He considered for an instant that everyone at sleep had that face, the same face the man's mother had probably seen when she put her sleeping baby boy to bed: blank and open, unstriped with what would come. The man did not awaken when they bent over him, but when they held his arms, once he felt their touch, he fought, fiercely throwing blows and trying to reach for the sharpened machete under his bed. The face was now contorted in rage and fear. Screaming. Puff-Puff stood at the door making suggestions, chuckling. The screaming continued. Then, Maximum walked past Puff-Puff and hit the man in the centre of the face with a large rock. The fight was over, and blood gurgled onto the mattress.

He could feel the sweat, cold, on his warm body. His palms were slick with moisture and red, and his eyes burned from the perspiration that dripped into them. There was noise now. Students waking up, muttering and yelling challenges from far away. He looked around the room and took in the tin plate with unfinished eba and a thin, congealed soup, the dwarf fridge, with an old rusted table fan on top. Suddenly, he felt cold. Maximum lifted the body onto his shoulder, and Puff-Puff led the way. Killer had driven the Cressida to the entrance of the dormitory hall. Seeing them, he opened up the trunk. Maximum threw the unconscious student in, almost as if he shrugged him off.

He was conscious of the other students in the shadows, cowering, watching them, of voices in the background attempting to organise resistance. Puff-Puff shoved him into the car and they sped off. He sat in the back, between Puff-Puff and Chinwendu. Killer drove.

As they drove on the curvy, lonely road away from the university, Puff-Puff was saying something, but all he could hear was Sade's slow, deceptive voice singing "Smooth Operator." He would later think to himself, perhaps, if that was all that happened that night, he might have forgotten. But it was not.

They killed the student in the trunk. They killed him under a tree, with the man on his knees, pleading. Maximum asked Killer to do it, with an old pistol unwrapped from within a bundle of chequered cloth like a gift. When Maximum spoke, the student stopped his screaming pleas and started sobbing, asking repeatedly, in a soft, plaintive voice: "Why?"

But Killer stood there, hesitating, asking questions about the gun, stalling. Puff-Puff walked up to the kneeling, trussed-up man, and slit his throat.

"I severed the common carotid artery. One time! Clinical," Puff-Puff would boast in the car.

The night was wearing on. The bar was now empty. The flies had left. "Please now, bring the beer!" Puff-Puff shouted at the serving girl. "You people are looking for my trouble!"

The serving girl smiled at him. Puff-Puff started to laugh, a shy laugh, almost like the giggle of a coy, flirty girl. "That small girl is looking for my trouble o," he sang. "One day, she will find what she is looking for."

"Na person wey craze man beat dey fear mechanic," Killer said, laughing. Puff-Puff chuckled in appreciation.

"What does that mean?" Chinwendu asked.

Puff-Puff eyed Chinwendu coolly, a small smile on his face.

"Chinwedu, you are a yeye man. You don't understand any jokes or proverbs. A mad man wears filthy clothing like a mechanic. If a mad man beat you, when you see mechanic, you go fear."

Chinwendu smiled. "Puff-Puff because you're now doing clinicals, that's why you are insulting me."

"Yes," Puff-Puff said, "soon, I will be a medical doctor. Is it easy?"

He sat back, sipping his beer. His conversation with Nnemka had been brief. "When are you coming back?" she had asked, her tone over the crackling phone line at the same time demanding and craven. It had irritated him, and he had hung up on her. On the way back to his fraternity brothers' table, he wondered if she was calling from inside his dorm room. She had once convinced his roommate to let her in. He found the thought pleasing.

When he returned to the table, Puff-Puff was speaking. "That's my private practice. For abortion, I dey charge 5k. If the girl fine I fit collect 2k, but I go poke first."

"Ol' boy, that's good money," Chinwendu said.

"Anyway," Puff-Puff said "this very fine babe come with 'im boyfriend. Something about the boy vex me. I can't even tell you what it was. And the boy come with the 5k complete." Puff-Puff stopped and looked into his beer, a wry smile on his face.

"I tell the boy: No!" Puff-Puff continued, "That I must poke the girl, then I will abort my own and the boyfriend own together."

Puff-Puff laughed. Killer and Chinwendu laughed. He laughed too. When the laughing stopped, Killer asked: "The boy agree?"

"The boy no know me," Puff-Puff said "'im wan' vex. Anyway, after a while 'im babe take am outside my flat dey beg am. The girl enter back inside without the boy, tell me say I go poke but say I go wear condom."

There was for a long moment silence around the table.

"I laugh, tell am say make 'im remove dress first." Puff-Puff took a swig from his bottle, savouring his timing like a trained comedian.

"Did you use the condom?" Chinwendu asked.

"For where?" Puff-Puff said "I poke am raw."

There was another silence. Then Killer laughed. "Wetin concern catfish with raincoat."

"O boy, you wicked o! " Chinwendu said, shaking his head and starting to chuckle.

"Na today you know?" Puff-Puff said, laughing.

He was standing at the end of Kofo Abayomi Street, waiting to catch a bus, when he saw Chinwendu pointing at him. Twelve years had passed since the night they met to drink after Maximum's funeral. A few other people had died since then. His mother was dead.

So was Puff-Puff. They had not kept in touch. After graduation, Puff-Puff had stayed in Enugu. He had moved to Lagos. He was reading the Vanguard one afternoon when he saw Puff-Puff's face staring at him from one of those purchased obituary notices captioned "Final Call" or "Glorious Homecoming" or "Call to Glory." This was almost eight years ago now. "Which sad event occurred November 23 at the University of Nigeria Teaching Hospital (UNTH) after a brief illness," the notice read. He had not attended the funeral.

"Cicero!" Chinwendu shouted, pulling his almost-new Toyota Camry over in traffic. "Enter, enter!" As he sat in the front passenger seat, Chinwendu leaned over and gave him an awkward hug; the seat safety belts got in the way. The music in Chinwendu's car was loud, pulsating.

They drove through Victoria Island turning into a bar at the end of a cul-de-sac in Lekki. He had never been there. It was the kind of bar that middle-class salaried men, office administrators, bankers, and lawyers, stopped at on their drive home from work.

The place was crowded. They found an open table in the back. The waitress knew Chinwendu and without being asked brought a cold bottle of Star, with the chill running down the sides like tears. He ordered a Guinness. An Arsenal and Wigan Athletic F.C. match played on the television propped on a wooden ledge against the wall. Below the TV was a display case. Behind its glass face, on metal shelves, lay meat pies, fried fish and grilled snails.

The case was lit by electric-blue fluorescent tubes. He saw a lone fly walking on the inside of the glass.

"How is Nnemka?" Chinwendu asked. He had married Nnemka and they had three children. His two sisters had also married. One happily, the other in a marriage like his. "She is fine," he answered.

Chinwendu had broadened, his cheeks heavy in a way that suited his angular face. He knew about Chinwendu's job at the bank, which gave him a good salary, supplemented by (or perhaps supplementing) the kickbacks and side deals he cut. He was conscious that Chinewndu was probably sizing him up in the same way, a prelude, he thought, to pity. Things had not gone well for him in Lagos. It had started well, and then changed.

He avoided their company. At first, consciously, then, after a time, by habit. He saw Chinwendu occasionally, but only because Chinwendu made the effort. Chinwendu was always offering to help. When his first job at the IT department of an insurance company ended abruptly, Chinwendu offered to get him a job at the bank where he worked. He had not attended the interview. He was on his way, in his suit, with a small attaché case when something - the taxi driver who wanted to overcharge him? a rude bus conductor? - had discouraged him, and he had returned to his house.

He was increasingly conscious of how he lived almost as an uninterested observer of his life. The sound of Nnemka's voice: *"I thought you were a man. A rugged guy. Look at your mates hustling, all of them doing well, driving big cars. You just sit here looking at me."*

"So, what are you doing now?" Chinwendu asked.

He told him he now ran his own company, providing IT support to small and mid-size companies. "My car broke down, but I had a job on the Island," he said in half-hearted explanation.

Chinwendu waved his arm as if dismissing the need for justification and lifted the beer glass to his lips. "When was the last time you saw Killer?"

"It's been long o! Over five years," he responded. "I hear he is doing very well."

"Doing well? The guy is rolling in money. But you know Killer's problem. He is too selfish. Too greedy and selfish. He's always been like that." Chinwendu was frothy as he described all the rules he bent at work to get Killer loans. "When it is time to give me my cut, Killer will start dribbling me, offering me peanuts."

They were silent for a while. The dull buzz of the football match filling the silence between them. Chinwendu spoke again. "Life is so funny. You won't believe who I saw the other day at the supermarket. Maximum's mother. I wouldn't have recognised her if she hadn't called me. The woman is old, and I don't think she is well."

"What did she say to you?" he asked.

"The same thing. That we are liars; that we know who killed Maximum." Chinwendu turned his gaze to the beer mug in his hand. "This life. All these years, how many times have I even thought about Maximum? He would never have entered my mind if I hadn't seen his mother."

After they had been drinking for three hours, Chinwendu dropped him off at a busy intersection where he could get a bus or taxi, and making a noisy U-turn, Chinwendu headed home to his family.

He noticed the pair of red-spotted, yellow butterflies flirting above the neat hedge of bougainvillaea flowers. Killer's gardener pushed the clattering lawn mower over the green grass, patches of sweat seeping through his light brown overalls. Occasionally, the clatter of stone and pebbles striking the mower's blades would come over the hum of the engine.

A bottle of white wine sat in the ice bucket on the white, cast iron garden table. Chinwendu lifted a frosted wine glass to his lips. "I can't bring myself to do it," Killer said.

Killer too was heavier now, his stomach distending in a modest paunch. He was also balding. When they arrived, Killer had given them a tour of his large house, dwelling on the media room with a giant screen and surround sound. Killer's wife, Fatima, stood at the edge of the dining room. "You are Cicero? Ndubisi has told me so much about you and your partying university days," she said, her pronunciation of Killer's name off, the emphasis on the wrong syllables.

Turning to Chinwendu, Killer said: "See how my wife dey greet Cicero, like say na better person." Chinwendu and Killer laughed. He laughed too.

Killer had been ebullient, showing off. His mood changed after they sat down on the patio and finished the second bottle of wine. "This bank examiner is giving me all kinds of problems. Now he is threatening to inform the police. He won't even collect bribe," Killer said. "I offered him thirty thousand dollars. Cash."

Chinwendu had been breezy, unconcerned. It was an examiner at another bank, not his. This was Killer's problem alone. "What did you do to the man? Why won't he take a bribe?" Chinwendu asked, smiling bitterly.

Killer's patio ensured seclusion. The sliding glass doors leading into the house were at a distance. As the evening advanced, the deck itself seemed to him eager to foster a conspiracy, pushing them closer as if in a huddle against the approaching darkness. When Killer's maid came to deliver another bottle of wine, they could hear her well before she got close.

Killer waited for the maid to walk back into the house before he said: "I have to deal with this situation decisively," his small eyes widened. Killer stopped looking at him and Chinwendu, and turned his eyes to the floor.

For a long time they drank in silence, cigarette smoke floating in the air. He could hear faint sounds from the rest of the house, Killer's children, wife, and a blaring television.

After the sun had set, Killer, out of the silence, as if speaking loudly to himself, said: "If you ask me why we killed that boy in Okigwe now, I can't tell you." Killer's face was set, his jaw pointing upwards. "Just wasted someone's life over some childish nonsense." In the reflected patio light, he could see Killer's eyes, morose, starting to cloud. Killer's shoulders dropped.

Then, Killer pulled himself up in his chair, looking over his manicured lawn in the direction of the garden statues, two cherubs with wings at their back and trumpets to their lips. "Here is a man that is a real threat to my family and me, and I can't do it."

It was late when they left. Killer walked them out to the driveway. Chinwendu lingered as they said goodbye, as if waiting to introduce another topic. Killer was impatient. "Ol' boy it's late. Let's see another time, abeg. Cicero, thanks for coming o. It's been long."

Chinwendu's Camry backed down the driveway slowly. When the car straightened on the road, Chinwendu drove off quickly, squealing the tires.

Chinwendu dropped him off at the bus stop along Ozumba Mbadiwe Street. He sat on the bus bench, bent over, his hands clasped between his knees. The night was still. Cars sped past, lights cutting into the darkness. Surprisingly, the street lights were working. The glowing orbs attracted things that circled the light, flying insects too far above for him to identify. He turned his face to the ground. On Killer's patio, with the three of them together, drinking, speaking loosely, he had thought of what they had been in university. The laughter, the camaraderie, the world opening up, as if by force to their collective spirit. The feeling he had, leaning against a car in Enugu, the evening starting to settle down, along with the harmattan dust, that he was entering a magical place, the place of men, where the things they wanted mattered and the world would bend to their will.

He thought of Killer's house, the driveway filled with cars, plastic children's toys scattered on the patio and Killer's tall wife. He thought of Killer's plodding walk, settling himself into a chair with a grunt. And Chinwendu's sharp eyes, filled with envy, always at the periphery, looking for the main chance. They were all that was left. They had killed two people at Okigwe, not one, he thought. Killer must have forgotten. But he remembered. He remembered everything that happened that night. Killer could forget. Killer had not been in that room. Killer had not killed anyone.

It was late. He had been waiting for a while. He had not seen a bus. He got up and started walking towards Lagos Island. Chinwendu should have offered to drive him home.

Expert in All Styles

I hear the neighbourhood roadside mechanic through the open back door. My mind is on the heat. I know from the prickly sensation on my forehead that I will soon start to sweat. "On it! On it!" the mechanic yells at someone I cannot see. The sound of the generator sputtering to life blows in from the open door. But the power doesn't come on. The fans don't turn, the fluorescent tubes don't light up, and the electric clipper is still dead in my hand. "Ok. Off it!" the mechanic shouts.

I hear clanking metal like he is beating a machine with a wrench. The generator starts buzzing, and the fluorescent lights blink. The fans begin to turn, slowly at first, then picking up speed till their blades are a whirling blur, and the rotating heads turn from one end of the salon to the other like mechanical busybodies.

"Oya now," my customer says from the chair, "finish quick before the light quench again." I put the buzzing clipper against his head and resume sculpting his fade. He is a regular. I don't like his smell, like rancid sweat topped off with one of those pungent colognes the hawkers sell in traffic. He comes in every two or three weeks to trim his hightop and fade. He is probably about my age - twenty-two or so. He works with computers. Doing what exactly, I don't know. All that is left now is trimming the thin line of hair that connects his scalp to his goatee. This is the part of the haircut he is most particular about. I change clippers, push his face back and put the edger on the line I mark with talcum powder. Young guys don't tip well. Some don't tip at all. This guy usually drops something. Two hundred or three hundred Naira. Enough to buy a Coke and cigarettes across the street when I take a break.

"You are a thief!" Boss is haggling with the mechanic. The mechanic shouts: "Oga, na work I do now! Workman no be thief." The five chairs in the salon are all occupied. It's busy like this on Saturdays. The customers come in waves. Boss puts some crumpled Naira bills into the mechanic's hand. The mechanic opens his palm to study the cash and then quickly closes it again and stuffs it deep into his trouser pocket. He starts to head for the front door. "I beg commot from back!" Boss yells. The mechanic stops, glances briefly at Boss perched on the stool from which he can see the barbers and the cashier, and moves to the open back door. "If generator quench again, make una call me. I still dey," the mechanic says as he leaves the salon. The mechanic shuts the back door, muting the rumble of the generator. "Useless man," Boss mutters to no one in particular, as he walks to his office.

"I beg Tochukwu, give me smoother," Umaru asks.

"Wetin do your own?" I respond as I hand him my smoother.

"I no know o. 'im just stop to work."

I try not to share my tools with the other barbers. But Umaru is ok. I focus when I do my work. Most of the other barbers don't. You can see it in small things, the casual way they handle clippers and blades. When I am finished with a cut, I remove my hands. It is done.

The fans are working well now. I can feel the heat being blown away. I hate to sweat. The computer guy admires his cut in the rectangular mirror I hold up to him. I move the mirror a little so that he can see the back of his head with the help of the long mirror that stretches the length of the salon. He nods quietly in appreciation. After paying the cashier, he walks back and squares me four hundred Naira, palming the money into my hand in a shake. He pulls me in close for a chest bump. It's something young guys do. Sometimes we put arms around each other's backs briefly. His funky stink fills my nostrils for a moment. Then he lets go and glides out of the salon, hitching up his cargo shorts with its bulging pockets as he passes the door.

Barbing takes work. You have to pay attention. To your customer, the lines you carve on their brows, and the graded thickness of the hair you leave behind. If you don't know, it looks easy. But you need talent, and then you need to focus. The customers notice. That is why sometimes there will be a line waiting for me while other barbers are open.

"Go to one of the free barbers now!" Boss will shout, exasperated, when a small crowd of young guys are waiting for me to give them a cut while the other barbers loiter. The young guys ignore him. If he catches someone's eye, they may say, "I am waiting for him," and point in my direction. Boss shakes his head in irritation. "Na the same thing now! How is his own different? It is the same haircut." Boss only talks like this to the young guys. Even though they are customers. The young guys don't budge. They wait for me.

It is almost 3 p.m. before I take a break. I am not complaining. When it is busy, I make money. I have to pay Boss rent for the chair every month. I give every customer a chit with my name for when they pay the cashier. When the Boss has earned his chair rent, we share what comes in eighty/twenty. I get eighty. Say what you like about Boss, but it's a better deal than anywhere else. Believe me, I have looked.

"Tobechukwu, bia, don't take too much time for your break. Customers will start coming again around four o'clock," he says to me in Igbo as I walk out the front door.

Boss insists on speaking to me in Igbo. I understand the language even though I can't speak very well. I am a Lagos boy. Born and half-bred, as my father would say. I am his only child. Born to his second wife, my Yoruba mother. He is dead now, but he left a long time before that. The morning after the night he nearly beat me to death. "I will kill you with my own hand first," he shouted, and my eyes were fixed on the thick tuft of grey and black hair that grew out of his ears before his blow landed and I lost consciousness. It is the last thing I remember of him. My mother cried, my battered, bleeding head in her lap. She was mourning the loss of a treasured husband.

Boss sometimes lends me some little money when I'm strapped. He doesn't do this for the other barbers. They are all Yoruba, except for Umaru, who is from Bauchi state.

"Madam, add more beans now! Ah, ah!" Umaru cries.

"E don do now!" the woman says, making a swift movement of her wrist, which carries little food to the plate.

I draw on my Benson & Hedges. Pulling the smoke through my nostrils. The best thing about Madam's Bukka is that there are no walls. The shed roof protrudes from a wall, held up by wood planks. The air can blow through. The breeze keeps you cool. We don't have to walk far. It is just across the street from the salon. "Oya, open the Coke now," I look up at the small girl that assists Madam on the weekends and evenings. "And bring two sachet Captain Jack."

I empty the alcohol into the Coke bottle. "You no go chop?" Madam asks. I ignore her. I pull again on my cigarette and then take a sip from my Coke bottle. Umaru does not close his mouth. You can see the food mashing together, brown and yellow.

I look into the street. Boss is trying to chase away the beggar. "Get out of here! You come here to disturb my customers every Saturday," Boss screams and tries to kick him. The beggar is crippled. He pulls away quickly on the board he powers with his arms. When he is a safe distance, he laughs. "God punish you!" he yells at Boss. Umaru looks up and laughs. His half-masticated food tumbles in his mouth. Boss stands on the street with his hands on his hips. He takes a few steps towards the beggar, and the beggar retreats a little further. Boss looks like he is gauging the distance to the beggar, then he abruptly turns back and walks to the salon.

"Yeye man! See am," Umaru says, jutting his chin towards Boss, who has passed through the salon door.

When we walk back to the salon, I square the beggar one hundred Naira. "Correct guy!" the beggar says. "Your boys are loyal!"

The big cars are starting to arrive. The wealthy men usually come in the evening. I look at the signs at the entrance. The one above the door reads "High Class Barbing and Beauty Salon," in black letters on a white board. The one beside the door is the one I like. In black, yellow and red letters: EXPERT IN ALL STYLES. Below the letters are sixteen painted silhouette heads with various dated hairstyles. The name of each cut is helpfully painted below each crudely drawn portrait. "Na correct sign be dis," I say to Umaru. He barely looks, grunts, and walks into the salon as I enter slowly behind him. The buzz of the alcohol is still in my ear.

The white fluorescent lights don't drive away the shadows falling through the windows from the setting sun. I look over to the long bench where the waiting customers are sitting and call, "Next." The older, wealthier customers come to the salon with their own clippers packed in black bags that look like oversized purses. Some hold them on their knees, and others let them dangle between their legs.

Umaru works next to me. We have two older men

in our chairs. They are in their mid or late sixties, older than the usual guys, even the wealthy ones. Close to my father's age when he died. There is very little hair to cut. I open the customer's black bag and take out an expensive clipper. He has his own combs and a barber's cape. I spread the barber's cape around his chest and shoulder with a flourish. As I fasten it over the wrinkled, folded, black-speckled brown skin at the back of his neck, I compliment him on the quality of his kit. He is balding, with grey, brown and black hair growing in an uneven crescent at the sides and back of his head.

Sometimes if you are good or if he just likes you, a wealthy customer will get your number and call you to come and barb him in his house. You can make a lot of money on these trips. Boss doesn't hassle too much, as long as you pay something meaningful toward the chair-rent when you get back. The man in my chair is rich. It's not just his kit; he smells clean, and his fresh cologne isn't hiding anything other than the smell of old flesh.

"Nze, I won't lie. That your Obiageli girl is beautiful. Asamkpete! Marvellous, wonderful hips and thighs. Elewu ukwu egbu ewu!" says the man in Umaru's chair.

"She is not a joke," the man in my chair chortles. The old men are speaking in Igbo.

"How much do you usually give her?"

"I see her only once a week. I give her five hundred

thousand Naira a month. I also help her with her rent every year. That one is two million," Nze says, turning his head slightly to Umaru's chair. I have to adjust the clipper to his sudden movement. There is very little noise in the salon. The sound of buzzing clippers and low conversation. I pause when I suddenly realise the old men assume I don't speak Igbo. They must imagine none of the people in the room understand what they are saying. I keep my face neutral.

"That's too much now!" the man in Umaru's chair exclaims. "Me, I don't pay anything like that amount o!"

"That's why you don't have your own Obaigeli and are admiring my own," Nze laughs. "At this age, only money is making us relevant. To these girls and anyone else o. I am happy to bring out the money, so I can enjoy my life."

"It's not a lie. Even my children, all they are calling me to discuss is for me to give them money," says Umaru's customer.

"All I do is send my children money. That is all they want from me. If my wife phones me, it's to complain about the money I am not sending her or someone else," Nze says, sighing.

Umaru is moving quicker on his customer's cut. He is tidying up the old man's sideburns. Occasionally, Umaru looks up at the football game playing silently on the small television in the corner. The man in his chair has a moustache to trim and shape. My customer, Nze, is clean-shaven. We will probably finish at about the same time.

"The young woman is too much. We finish one round, and she tells me she wants another. That I should lift her up against the wall and do it. I told her if that is what she wants, I can call my houseboy from downstairs to do it," Nze says, leaning forward in the chair. His friend laughs. I slow down the clipper and clean up the back of his neck. My neck is starting to itch. "If she is looking for someone to kill, it's not going to be me," he adds, laughing. His friend laughs too.

His friend whistles, "So you just do that one round for one hundred thousand Naira."

"It is ok for me. Once a week. It is enough," he says.

"There is something I will give you to drink. Just one cup, and you will do three or four rounds. Trust me," his friend says.

"Don't give me. I won't drink," Nze says. "The one round I am doing is ok for me. And I know what I am swallowing to get it." Both men are laughing now. Involuntarily, I also start smiling, my lips parting slightly in front of my white teeth.

"This boy understands Igbo," Umaru's customer says, turning to me. They are still speaking in Igbo.

"Come, this boy, what is your name?" Nze says, turning and lifting his face towards mine.

"Tobechukwu," I repy.

They start laughing. "And you have just been quietly listening to us," Umaru's customer says.

"Don't mind the stupid boy," Nze says, laughing playfully. "You won't even know he is an Igbo boy," he says as he turns again and looks at me slowly.

Umaru and I carry the black bags with our customers' kit out the front door. We walk behind the old men to their black SUVs parked on the street. When we reach Nze's, Umaru continues walking behind the other man. I see the beggar swing in behind them, paddling furiously and calling out. As Nze climbs into the driver's seat, he takes the black leather purse from me. "Tobechukwu, what is your number?" he asks. He types the digits into his iPhone. The car's interior is a greyish-white. Before he closes the door, he grunts and squares me five thousand Naira. "Ah, Chief! Thank you! Please flash me so I will have your number," I say. He nods. As the SUV starts to pull away, I see his number flash for a couple of rings on my phone, then die. I am saving the number when Umaru slides next to me. "My guy try o. 'Im sort me 1k," he says. "My guy try pass o. Na 2k 'im sort me," I lie, pushing my phone back into my trousers.

We don't close the salon till it's almost ten o'clock.

Boss's Hi-Ace bus carries us to the Mainland. I sit near the back with the window open. The cashier sits in front, near the driver. The other barbers sit around her.

"You dis girl, you fine o!

"I beg no dey disturb am o. Na my girlfriend o."

"Which kind girlfriend? Na my wife."

"For where?"

"Dey there now! My papa people don carry wine, pay bride price for 'im head."

"You sabi where your papa dey?"

"Make you still dey talk. We don go her village. I beg Chinwe make you tell dis yeye boys."

"Make una leave me, I beg. Na barber money una wan' take marry me?"

"God punish you Chinwe for saying that!"

I inch my head out of the window so I can feel the wind on my face. I don't say anything.

When I get off at Gbagada, Chinwe says "You no follow dey toast me?"

"Na fine boy dey worry am," one of the other barbers says.

"I know my level now," I say, as I get off.

I walk away quickly from the bus. I don't go to the small flat I share with four roommates. I breathe the air, catching the cooling night in my nostrils, along with the paraffin fumes blowing from the fires of the night market women. I stop and buy cigarettes and a bottle of Captain Jack. I look for the text on my phone with the address for tonight. My mother's missed call is on the phone. She only calls me on the weekends. I rarely call back. Things are rough for her. She usually wants money. I only call back when I can help. I find the text.

I am high on alcohol and some laced weed. The small hotel room is humid, packed with bodies, the old-style airconditioner impotently droning in the corner. The fluorescent lights flicker, casting purple shadows on the slow-moving bodies. My nostrils open and fill the back of my head with the sweet, musty stink of cigarette smoke, sweat and spilt alcohol. The door is open, and some of the men stand outside in the long balcony, a flexible barrier, making way as more men walk through the door. Everyone is sweating. A man walks in wearing a fishnet singlet and a green jacket, with a gold-coloured purse slung over his shoulder. The music suddenly comes on again. I kiss the one standing next to me. The saliva tastes stale in my mouth.

(2)

I trim the backside of Nze's head, clipping the hairs that run down the back of his neck through to his shoulder. The clipper purrs steadily.

"Where is your father from?" he asks. I tell him.

"But he is late," I add.

"I am sorry. When a boy's father dies, he becomes a man," he says.

"We didn't get along. He left my mother many years before he died," I lie. Perhaps it is only a half-lie. It is close to the truth. He left my mother to rid himself of me. A large split-unit air conditioner cools the room, barely humming in the background. I feel cool, the airconditioner extracting both heat and humidity.

"He had a problem with you?" Nze asks. He looks at me with wide-open eyes. I see tiny specks of yellow and brown in his eyeballs. Then he turns his face from me, his nostrils flaring, their openings thick with grey-black hair. The old guys have this a lot. Hair growing aggressively from strange places. I don't respond.

The bedroom is large and white. The bed linen is white. The floor is a red-clayed tile with protruding patterns that look like minarets. Nze sits on a dining room chair draped with a white bedsheet. His houseboy, a slender man about my age, sweeps up hair with a short broom and a red plastic dustpan.

"I can't say I blame him. Most people don't understand," Nze says suddenly. He shifts, adjusting his weight and then settles deeper in the chair. I use small scissors to clip the hairs that sprout from his ears like a starburst of grey lines. He is quiet for a few minutes, and then he says, "You have to find your own way."

"He used to beat me. Even when I be small boy. Like say if 'im see me e go vex am," I say. "He was a bastard." Nze barely moves. He looks at the houseboy and then at me. "Don't talk about your father like that," he says. I don't respond.

After I finish Nze's cut, I rub hemp oil into his scalp, massaging the folds of skin on his head, from the back and sides to the crown. I can hear him sigh, and his shoulders fall.

"Very good, very good," Nze hums. He sits still for a moment, barely moving, and suddenly springs from the chair. "Haven't you finished?" he barks at the houseboy. The houseboy stares back, catching his eye. Nze looks away. "Go and prepare breakfast," he orders and turns away. I am packing the clipper and combs into the black purse. The houseboy walks out of the door, closing it gently behind him.

"Please wait for me. Let me take a shower. Then I will look for the money to pay you," Nze says.

I sit on the white bed, looking at the white walls. The door to the bathroom is ajar. I can hear the sound of the shower and Nze fiddling with containers. The steam starts to puff through the doorway in grey curling wisps. When he is done, Nze comes out of the bathroom in a white bathrobe. He walks over to the bed and sits beside me. "Please, young man," he says, his eyes fixed on mine "you will help me rub my shoulder."

Nze is sleeping. The hair on his chest and stomach is a carpet of matted grey and black curls. His skin folds in rigid waves over his paunch, rising and falling with each breath. I lift his arm off my abdomen and pull on my trousers.

I look around the cool, clean room. My mother lives in a dirty, smelly compound at the edges of Katangowa. I only go there when I have money to give her. As soon as I get to her compound I have the urge to leave. Her teeth are rotting in her mouth. When I say I am leaving she smiles and tries to hold my hand. I need to smoke. I put on my shoes and glance at Nze. His face is buried in the white pillows.

The houseboy opens the large wooden door and lets me out of the house. He barely looks at my face. Nze's gateman holds open the black compound gate as I walk through. The gateman's eyes scan my face. I stop to catch his eyes. He looks away. The gate is slammed shut behind me with a loud, heavy clang. I start to walk to the main street where I can get a taxi. I quicken my pace. I don't think of my father often. But as I cross the street, I am thinking of him and his forearm, carpeted in grey and black hairs, raised to strike me. I have one hundred thousand Naira in my pocket and tears, I think, in my eyes.

The Lake Chad Club

The dust hung in the air, powdering the drying grass and settling on the white paint on the concrete kerbs that marked the roads around the faculty buildings. In the parking lot, their father's Peugeot's doors stood ajar, as if it had been abandoned abruptly by fleeing passengers.

A few metres away, across the parking lot, in the roundabout, the children sat on the landscaped lawn beneath a mango tree whose branches spread out to the edges of the traffic circle. The boy was barking at the tree, "Halima! Halima! Come down. You know you shouldn't be climbing trees." His younger sister, her oval face emerging from a laurel of green mango leaves browned with light dust, smiled down, revealing the gap between her front teeth. "Ismailia, come and get me out of the tree. Or are you afraid?"

Ismailia looked up at the tree, unsure of what to do next. Azeeza, his older sister, sat on the grass, her floral dress stretched over her knees. She glanced up, her left hand cupped over her eyes to protect them from the sun. "Halima, come down. When we get home, I will tell mama that you have been climbing trees again, and she will beat you." Azeeza looked away from the tree and her sister and passed her left hand through her hair. Halima ignored Azeeza and stuck her tongue out at her brother.

"Come down from that tree, Halima." Professor Mohammed Kyari called out, his voice slightly impatient but half-distracted. He had suddenly appeared at the car door, surprising the children who had been waiting an hour in the mid-morning sun for him to finish work in the office. Professor Kyari wore a suit, a white shirt and a tie. He dressed formally whenever he came to the University of Maiduguri Teaching Hospital, even on a Saturday like this one. Cradled in his arm were manila-coloured files and a doctor's coat that looked unnaturally white in the brilliant sun. Professor Kyari placed the files and the carefully folded coat on the front passenger's seat without looking again at his children. He tapped distractedly on the steering wheel with his long, charcoal-black fingers. Azeeza, Ismailia, and Halima ran into the back of the car, slamming the doors shut behind them. Without looking back at the children, Professor Kyari started the car and began the drive out of the Teaching Hospital.

Halima leaned forward and poked her head between the front seats. Her hair was in a ponytail, and the green bow her mother had pinned to her hair was slightly askew. She raised herself to an almost standing position. "Are we going to the Lake Chad Club?" she asked her father. Her mouth opened into a smile as he looked back at her.

"Yes, Habibti. Inshallah, after I buy some things in the market, we will go and pick up your mother," Professor Kyari replied.

"Where else do we go on Saturdays?" Azeeza asked rhetorically, pushing away from her seat and looking out the window at two female students strolling on the sidewalk. Azeeza was fourteen years old, and Halima was eight, and Azeeza thought it important to keep a distance between her longing for the Lake Chad Club and her younger sister's childish desires.

Azeeza kept looking at the students, turning back to focus on the style of their jeans, which clung tightly to their bodies in a fashion that was suddenly in vogue. Azeeza was transfixed as the tall young woman started to laugh, her lips lined by a deep red lipstick, and threw her head back, her hair, in small braids, falling behind her.

"Please sit down Halima," Professor Kyari said, "I am driving fast."

Ismailia pulled Halima into the back seat, tugging at the belt of her dress. Halima hit him on his hand as she fell back, her face pouted in defiance and rage. Ismailia shouted "Walahi, I will beat you!"

"Leave your sister alone," his father said quietly, without turning back to look at them.

When they drove into the grounds of the Lake Chad Club, Mrs. Kyari was seated in the passenger seat. Professor Kyari's medical files had been placed in the Peugeot's boot, and his white medical coat transferred to a wooden hanger on the back of the master bedroom door in the family's three bedroom senior staff bungalow.

Mrs. Kyari is a large woman, with many curves and folds, and light brown skin, and curly hair that fell to the middle of her back, when she oiled and combed it out on Sunday evenings while she waited for her husband's return from the club. On Sundays, after her evening bath, she would apply a perfumed shea butter infused with cloves and cocoa beans to her soft skin as she sang to herself waiting for the sound of the Peugeot throttling up the curved drive. Their bedroom would be filled with the scent of a heady incense she burned in censers made of occluded silver and decorated with elaborate, cryptic, carvings. She inherited the censers from her mother, a formidable Shuwa Arab trader, along with formulas for incense and keen briefings on a man- a husband's - needs. None of this could be discerned as she sat in the car, her scarf tightly fixed around her head, framing her beautiful, plump face, and falling to the shoulders of her large formless gown, her eyes and her mouth set in a tight smile.

The car had barely stopped before the children jumped out. Halima and Ismailia ran towards the play area where gales of laughter rose and fell from the merry-go-round, swings and see-saws clustered in a tight circle, their leather sandals making prints in the whitish brown sand. The trees on the club grounds provided a high canopy that deflected the burning sun, and Azeeza strolled slowly towards the table tennis pavilion where the teenagers were standing around with bottles of Coke and Fanta in their hands, watching a game between two boys wearing football jerseys. She shuffled the curls in her shoulder-length hair with her left hand and bobbed her head in the way she had seen in a Madonna video. Azeeza quickly scanned the group of eleven or so teenagers to see if Abbai was there. Then she saw him, leaning back against one of the pillars that held up the roof of the table tennis shed, his left foot lightly placed on the wall behind him. He was looking down at the ground, and then, almost like magic, he looked up at her and smiled.

Professor Kyari held an arm out to his wife, and she leaned on him as she lifted her frame from the car. When they had first been married, she had been surprised, and a little embarrassed, by these little attentions. With time, she had come to cherish deeply the little ways he acknowledged his affection for her in public. It was not the open and unsubtle ways she saw some of the other couples hold and kiss at the Lake Chad Club, especially the European and American women.

Professor Kyari watched his wife walk ahead of him towards the club entrance, the curves of her large body as she moved, concealed, yet discernable, through her loose robes, stirred him. She stopped at the board at the entrance that read: NAMES OF PAST PRESIDENTS OF LAKE CHAD CLUB, MAIDUGURI AND THE YEARS THEY SERVED. As they always did since the end of her husband's tenure at the beginning of the year, her eyes stopped on the last entry: "Prof. Mohamed Kyari 1984–1986"

Dateline: Maiduguri, June 9, 2015: The spokesman for the Borno State Governor, Alhaji Mustapha Umaru, announced today that the Federal Government was reopening Maiduguri International Airport to passenger and commercial traffic. "I am happy to inform you that Maiduguri airport has been reopened. The airport was shut down on December 2, 2013 following a deadly attack on a military base and air force base near the airport. We have received a letter from the Chief of the Airforce to that effect. In fact, a commercial airline has indicated interest in commencing flight operations soon" he stated. In his statement the Governor's spokesman praised the Nigerian Military for the patriotism and the bravery it has exhibited in the face of the unrelenting Boko Haram onslaught. He urged the citizens of the State to continue to give all support to the counter-insurgency operation.

The children decided that Halima would be the first to go to claim the body. She was her father's favourite, they all knew, but the reason her siblings gave was more practical: She lived in Abuja and was closest. Ismailia would be coming in on Wednesday from Lagos. Azeeza, coming in on connecting flights from London, would arrive on Friday just in time for *Salat al-Janazah* prayers. Halima was running late. She told her driver to speed up. She was afraid she would miss her flight. She was taking the flight alone. Her husband and three children would stay in Abuja. She was filled with sadness that she could barely begin to understand when she thought of her father's death. She had asked him to leave. He would not go. He said it was his home. It seemed incomprehensible to her that he was dead and that he died when she was not by his side. His face, full of pride and concern when he turned to her, was her definition of love. She was barely aware of the ways she sought that look in the face of the man that married her. When her husband told her the news, looking pensively at her and then at his phone, she felt cold. As if a door had closed, trapping her in a frigid, frozen world.

She reached into her handbag to ensure her tickets and scarf were there. She would need to wear a hijab in Maiduguri.

The night was clear and sharp and the air still and dense, barely disturbed by the raindrops that fell like reluctant tears, starting and stopping, with the unpredictable rhythm of recalled grief. The rain barely wet the ground. The night had slowly eclipsed the day, the sun laying for a long time in a low line of striking orange and brown clouds as the far-off calls to the *Mahgrib* prayers echoed. The teenagers barely noticed. They took turns playing table tennis in mixed pairs, speaking in groups of three or four.

"I am named after the Nile, at least what the Ethiopians call it. My mother named me," Abbai said. He was quiet for a moment. "She became a professor before my father. In Egypt, before we came to Nigeria." He was still looking down at his feet. Then as if he had remembered something, he added, "She has a degree in Near East Studies from Princeton."

"My mother didn't go to university. Though you would never know, the way she tells everyone what to do," Azeeza said. She was looking at Abbai's long thin face. His skin was the colour of a brown olive, and as he laughed at her comment, his white teeth exploded onto his face. He had an overbite and was conscious of his smile. He quickly closed his mouth, but a smile lingered in the corners of his mouth.

They stood slightly apart from the rest of the group. Azeeza had her handbag slung across her chest, and as she spoke, she played with its thin leather strap.

In a sudden panic of self-consciousness, she looked up, scanning the pavilion, looking to see if any of the other teenagers were focused on her and Abbai. She had known most of them for years. They were children of academics that worked at the university like her father or of a few of the leading civil servants, lawyers and businessmen. Some of them were Nigerians, some were Europeans, some, like Abbai, had parents from other parts of Africa, and a few of them were mixed race. A very few were the mysterious children of senior military officers, who seemed to be raised in a very different way. No one seemed to be paying attention to Abbai and her. She moved a little closer to Abbai. He was wearing a cologne, the scent wafting and waning as if riding on an imperceptible wind that blew between them.

"Let's go to the pool," Abbai said, tilting his long head in its direction.

"But it's dark, no one's there," Azeeza replied.

"Let's go and see," Abbai's voice faltered.

Ismailia held on to the large standing swing. The children were gathered in opposing camps on each platform, doing their best to go as high as possible. The competition was heated. Some of the nannies had joined in the game, clamouring as the swing flew high into the night sky, carrying the joyful, terrified, screams of the children. Behind Ismailia, the two boys he considered his best friends held on, squished so close that there was barely any space between them. They pushed and pulled with all their strength as some of the younger children began to scream in genuine terror. He could feel Lateef pressed against his back, Lateef's lips shouting into his ear, "Higher! Let's go higher!!" Lateef was one of the military children. His father was the Military Governor of Borno State.

The women sat in a circle of hastily pooled tables in the small garden that led off the side of the main club building. They were making plans for the annual bazaar. Their practised ears clearly picked up the conversation over the loud shrieks of the children. Mrs. Kyari wore a scarf loosely over her hair. She was the only woman at the Lake Chad Club who covered her head.

"We will make this bazaar bigger," Mrs. Kyari said. "Let us invite some of the craftswomen to make a stand.

We can charge them for a tent. They will be happy to pay."

"Should we really be charging them?" Mrs. Okonkwo, a Dutch woman married to an Igbo Microbiologist asked.

"Why not?" Mrs. Kyari asked dismissively. "That's how we raise money. Trust me, they will be making money too. A lot of money," she laughed.

Just then, a particularly loud shriek caused Mrs. Okonkwo to glance over, nervously, at the play area. "Don't worry Lotte," Mrs. Kyari said. "They won't be able to kill themselves."

Mrs. Kyari was conscious of the fact that most of the wives at the club had the formal education she lacked. She has adapted to this in various ways, and as time passed, she dominated the club in much the same way her mother had dominated the merchant women of Borno. Although she initially felt self-conscious that she alone wore a scarf, she could not bring herself to abandon the most visible manifestation of the habit of outward modesty that her mother had driven in to her. As time went by, she began to feel that the scarf and her character combined to lend her an authority that she may not have so readily secured with these spectacularly well-educated women.

A devout woman raised in a strict way by a formidable woman, it is perhaps more accurate to say

Mrs. Kyari never even considered abandoning the scarf. She could be pushed by the expectations of those around her, her husband's modern ways for instance, to loosen the customs she had grown up with in other ways – to let her daughter Azeeza, who was long past the age when she should be wearing a veil, wear tight jeans and put on make-up, leaving her hair uncovered- but not to alter her own deeply ingrained habits. Everyone around her, her husband, her children, the women she bought cloth from in the markets, the other women at the club, all seemed in subtle, irrefutable ways, to be making an argument, to be moving away quickly from these old customs and it appeared right to her that this should be the case. She felt it right that her daughter Azeeza would not be compelled to cover her hair in a veil at seven the way that she had been. In this way, over the years she had loosened her scarf and now sometimes wore it loosely over her hair so that her dark curls could be seen where it sprouted from her brow and temples.

Halima swayed on the metal seated swing. Its end-posts were almost perfect triangles, joined by a red-painted metal shaft on which evenly spaced chains of metal hung, linked at the ends by dark wooden seats. The younger children played on these swings. Halima, seated on the short wooden bench, tried to throw herself higher and further in the air. She wanted to go as high in the air as the older children on the standing swing. When she couldn't, she became restless, jumped off and approached the standing swing. Her brother waved her off. Halima, furious, stood dangerously close to the swing, in protest.

"This your sister is too stubborn!" Lateef yelled in Ismailia's ear. "Don't you people beat her at home?" Ismaila could feel Lateef's breadth, hot and moist in his ear. He pulled one arm away from the swing and waved Halima away again. Halima tried to reach out an arm to smack her brother but one of the nannies caught her around the waist and pulled her away from the fast moving swing. Immediately the nanny let her go, Halima ran away into the darkness, towards the line of *Dogan Yaro* and *Gmelina* trees. No one watched her as she ran and as she moved faster she felt free and happy and when she was by the tree line she was out of breath and overjoyed.

Halima climbed quickly into the crook of a *Dogan Yaro* tree in the darkness, her feet easily finding footholds in a tree she had climbed innumerable times. Once in the tree, she could see the entire back of the club - the concrete screen of the outdoor cinema, the pool lights that lit up the empty swimming pool. She sat in the tree, enjoying the freedom of being alone and doing what she wanted to do. She knew she risked her mother's anger. Azeeza had told their mother Halima climbed the mango tree at the University Teaching Hospital and her mother had wanted to spank her. But Professor Kyari had intervened, ordering Mrs. Kyari to leave Halima alone. "You will spoil this girl rotten Habibi. How can a girl her age be climbing trees? If no one beats her she will not stop." Mrs. Kyari complained. But her husband had already left the living room to change into the short sleeved safari suit he usually wore to the club.

Halima glared at Azeeza. Although Halima was more careful about a direct confrontation with her elder sister than she was with her brother, she felt furious, incomprehensibly betrayed, and mouthed "I will get you!" Azeeza avoided Halima, looked in the mirror and fixed her hair. She tried to ignore Halima's furious face, still hovering around the mirror, trying to catch her eye.

The pool area was deserted and dark. The only light came from the pool lamps that lit up the water with a whitish blue luminescence and cast a shifting metalized glow on their faces, as if they were at a table in a night club lit with strobe lights. Abbai had rolled up his trousers and placed his feet in the water. Azeeza sat beside him, her shoulders resting on his arms, her knees bent and her feet planted on the blue tiles that lined the edge of the pool. Azeeza felt Abbai caressing her arm with his hand. It felt uncomfortable. He had been playing with the water, and his hand was wet and cold. But it was getting warmer. He started kissing her neck. She was not sure what to do. She was afraid that someone might see them. But she was also warm and excited, as his kisses around her neck started to move to her cheeks. She turned around to face Abbai. Then she kissed him fully on the lips, his open mouth hungrily receiving hers. The kiss lingered, and she was unsure of what to do next. She could feel Abbai's right hand start to rub the side of her body. She could feel his hand, slowly, tentatively climbing up her side and chest until he had cupped his palm around one of her breasts. The hand lay there for a moment as if it was unsure what to do next.

They were in this position for a few moments and then Abbai started to reach his hand under her blouse. At that moment Azeeza, filled with both desire and dread, panicked and screeched. The sound shocked them both. They looked up and then around them to see if anyone had heard. It was then that they saw Halima, who had climbed down from the tree, watching them from the other side of the pool.

Halima's eyes, Halima's mouth with the gap between her front teeth, both were open and amazed, lit with the neon-like, ethereal glow of the reflected pool water lights. "I am going to tell Mama," Halima declared before Azeeza could speak, and took off in a full run towards the play area. Azeeza pushed Abbai away and ran after her sister.

In the glow of the club light and the outside lamps, Halima could make out the silhouette of her mother seated with her friends in the garden beyond the play area. She looked back when she heard her sister screaming her name and saw that Azeeza was swiftly catching up with her.

At that moment, Azeeza saw the large standing swing hit Halima and throw her up in the air. Halima landed in the whitish-brown dirt with a dull thud. Halima did not move. There was an almost instant, collective scream and suddenly everyone and everything was quiet. Halima was still not moving. The nannies were the first to start screaming again.

Dateline: Maiduguri, 24 Jul 2017: Numerous casualties have been reported in attacks on two internally displaced persons camps in Maiduguri by female suicide bombers. The disclosure was made by one Abdulrahman, a civilian self- defense group spokesman. The attack which involves over eight killed is the latest such attack in Maiduguri, the Northeastern Nigeria city that is the birthplace of Boko Haram. Boko Haram has increasingly targeted the city with suicide bombers and lately has specialized in using female bombers. Although Nigeria's government recently declared the group "crushed," dozens of attacks have since taken place. This latest bombings took place shortly after Nigeria's army chief of staff issued a 40-day deadline to his troops to "flush out Boko Haram's leader and finish off the group." Over the last eight years Boko Haram attacks have killed more than 20,000 people. It has created one of the world's largest humanitarian crises with thousands kidnapped, millions dislocated from their homes and spreading food insecurity.

Ismailia had made up his mind to go to Maiduguri. It was his duty. He found it difficult to maintain this decision. Now that his sisters were on their way, the decision could not be unmade. He could not think of his father's death for long and remain sober. He had hoped that they would have had an opportunity to speak again. He had always imagined that he and his father would have a reconciliation before his father died (or he died, in this life, who knows who goes first). He thought his father was an open and fair man, to many others but he felt, not to him. His alienation from his father had been a sore point with his sisters. They urged him to reconcile with him, "Don't be stubborn, whatever you have done, ask him for forgiveness." But of course, they didn't know what caused the rift with their father and he would never tell them. Lateef had volunteered to drive him to the airport. Lateef hugged him tightly and patted him on the back. He walked into the domestic flights terminal at the

Lagos airport with his ticket in his right hand. He had a small carry-on bag in his left.

The night sky was clear and the moon had grown large, glowing like a white phosphorous ball in a bed of dark wool. It was just past the time for *Isha* prayers and it was quiet. No muezzin called. Beside the phosphorous moon, white clouds, like the cornrows jet airlines make in the sky, arranged themselves in parallel lines. It was a remarkable sight, but no one was looking at the sky. They had gathered around Halima and formed a circle where she lay. Azeeza was on her knees bent over her sister. She called out Halima's name but her sister did not respond.

Mrs. Kyari was cursing the devil as she ran to her daughter. She shifted her weight rapidly from one foot to the other, but the effect it produced was a waddle with a stilting gait that caused a few of the older boys, watching her approach at the outer edges of the circle, to chuckle, hiding their mouths behind their hands. The circle parted for Mrs. Kyari. Halima still had not moved. Her eyes were closed. Mrs. Kyari wails rent the air. It was Abbai who lifted Halima and carried her in measured steps into the main building of the Lake Chad Club. Mrs. Kyari kept up by his side, smoothing her daughter's hair and reciting the One Hundred and Twelfth Surah of the Qur'an about the absolute supremacy of God.

The clamour of the praying, wailing, party brought Professor Kyari and many of the grand gentlemen of the club to the entrance door. He rushed to his daughter, gently taking him from the young boy's arms, cradling her and taking care, not to move her neck more than was necessary. His eyes looked carefully at her from the top of her forehead to her abdomen which heaved gently, partly exposed where her blouse was crunched up around her belly. He carried her into the billiards room where only a few moments ago a spirited game had been taking place between Dr. Okonkwo ("merely a PHD," as was the half-jest in the medical faculty for all non-medical doctors) and Professor Abdullah, an expert in Arabic literature. Professor Abdullah, seeing Professor Kyari approach and guessing his intention, cleared the remaining billiard balls with one sweep of his cue stick, scattering the balls to the far corners. Then Professor Kyari laid Halima on the green felt top of the table. Mrs. Kyari, seeing her daughter lying still on the large table, cried out: "They have killed my child."

"She is breathing. She is alive," Professor Kyari said quietly to his wife, as he forced open Halima's eyelids and judged the pupils' reaction to the bright lights that hung above the billiards table. The bright lights shocked and blinded Halima and caused her to sit up abruptly. She had regained consciousness when Abbai was carrying her into the club. The first thing she had been conscious of was the offensive odour of Abbai's cologne and then in rapid succession, her father's voice thanking the boy (for what?) his voice dripped in concern, her mother's voice praying, then her father's arms holding her, carrying her. She kept her eyes shut, biding her time, trying to discern what was going on in the world, until her father's fingers pried them open.

"Halima, Habibti, are you ok?" her father asked, looking at her closely, the features of his face filled with both relief and concern.

"Baba, my head hurts," Halima said, reaching out to touch the right side of her head.

"Someone get her some water to drink," her father ordered, speaking to no one in particular.

"I want Fanta," Halima said, and a dozen men around the billiard table, all her father's friends, or men who held him in great esteem, roared with laughter. Professor Abdullah repeated her words to some of the older members who had not heard Halima's comment close to the bar. This set off another round of laughter, smaller and more muted. The club steward appeared swiftly, almost magically, with a Fanta bottle, cold beads of water running down its side. Halima sat up on the pool table with the Fanta bottle in both hands. She looked around, at the Billiards Room Booking Board, the wood-panelled ceiling, the large white fan that dropped from the roof, and at her father who was now sitting beside her on the billiard table. It was a few minutes before she put the Fanta bottle to her lips.

The club steward and the assistant stewards, dressed in their white shirts, black trousers and bowties, started to disperse the crowd of teenagers and children that had wandered into the bar and the billiards room. They knew they were in a forbidden space and left quickly.

The women started to wander out to the garden on their own, except Mrs. Okonkwo who had taken a seat beside her husband at the bar and began to drink a beer.

Mrs. Kyari satisfied herself that her daughter was well by placing her daughter's face between her hands and asking Halima if she was ok. Halima nodded, moving her head up and then down slowly. "Alhamdulillah," Mrs. Kyari said, touching Halima's face. "You nearly gave me a heart attack," she added in English. Halima smiled. The phrase sounded odd, almost funny, coming out of her mother's mouth. Mrs. Kyari, elated with relief, winked at her daughter, participating in the joke. She ran her finger through Halima's hair and walked out of the billiards room intent on conducting an inquisition to find the servant whose negligence had led to the accident.

As she walked past the bar, on her way to the garden, she noted with a shudder Mrs. Okonkwo drinking at the end of the bar. She knew almost all the men in the club drank, even the Muslims. However, she simply could not comprehend why any woman would drink in public. She was grateful. Her husband never drank, neither in the club nor in private. Her children were healthy, and her life was full and joyful. She was grateful to God. If she had a niggling worry, it was because her husband did not say his prayers. She felt this as a vulnerability, a path through which evil and misfortune might enter their lives. She had tried to bring it up several times early in the marriage. Her husband's response had been firm and flat: "There is no compulsion in religion."

Professor Kyari sat in a large leather armchair with his daughter in his lap. The steward had delivered the chicken and chips Halima asked for and she ate quietly as she watched the men playing billiards, laughing and talking in their deep animated voices. The men would smile at her and pat her head when they passed by the leather chair. Professor Abdullah offered her a spicy sweet that he took from a deep pocket in his tunic and told her that her name meant she was gentle and generous and many men would write poems about her. "As she sings poetry; whose every note; moves hearts to fly; to their *lote* tree," he recited, closing his eyes as he spoke.

Halima was not sure she understood most of what he said but she liked the savoury sweet and wondered if she could ask for another. Professor Kyari watched her closely, sometimes rubbing the right side of her face and asking her if she could see things clearly. He seemed suddenly curious about the sorts of things he hardly paid attention to. Asking Halima the name of her teacher, and the names of her friends and silly questions like how many States were in Nigeria and the capital of Borno State. "Baba but you know it's Maiduguri," she laughed. "Everyone knows that Baba."

"What is the last thing you remember before you got here Habibti?" Professor Kyari asked.

"I wanted to play on the swing but they wouldn't let me, Baba," Halima answered.

She was happy sitting there in her father's lap listening to his voice and the strange voices of his friends. She didn't feel like going outside, running or climbing trees. She wanted ice cream. Professor Kyari called the club steward and passed on the request.

Outside, his path lit by the large moon, Ismailia ran after Lateef past the pool and into the trees. He was furious. Lateef had just said that his mother ran like a duck. Another friend ran after them calling their names and asking them to stop. When they crossed the line of *Gmelina* trees, Lateef turned round to face Ismailia, a sneer on his face. Ismailia threw a wild punch at him and missed. Lateef grabbed Ismailia around the legs with his arms and threw him to the ground. He pulled himself above Ismailia, who was trying to swing at him with his arms. Lateef held Ismailia's hands to the ground pinning him to the earth with Lateef's weight resting on Ismailia's waist. Ismailia heaved, trying to throw Lateef off him.

Lateef laughed. "You see! You are not strong! Do you think you are a big man? Are you a soldier?" Lateef was still laughing as he reached for Ismailia crotch. "Release your soldier! Let's see."

The third boy caught up with them. Lateef slid his fingers away from Ismailia's jean zipper and rolled off his friend. "Please don't fight," the third boy said. "Let's all be friends."

Dateline: Maiduguri, 26 June 2018: On Saturday, June 25, Boko Haram continued its attacks on the University of Maiduguri campus and environs with a series of suicide bombings. The latest attack was the eighth in the past six months. Professor Mohammed Kyari, a former dean of the Faculty of Medicine and an Emeritus Professor of the university, was killed while performing his early morning prayer in a mosque that was targeted by suicide bombers during one of the attacks. Giving details on the June 25 attack, Borno State Commissioner of Police, Clement Nwachukwu, confirmed that 16 people, including the UNIMAID professor, were killed while 13 others were injured when multiple suicide bombers gained entry into the university campus. Nwachukwu lamented the security loopholes which permitted the attacks and marred the robust arrangements made by the police and other security agencies, which led to the peaceful conduct of recent Sallah across the state. He said the desperate suicide bombers, who were denied access to soft targets and prayer grounds, took advantage of the night to penetrate the university and detonate their Improvised Explosive Devices (IEDs), unleashing mayhem.

Azeeza steeled herself for the search as she approached the security line in Terminal Five at Heathrow. The manner of her father's death had shocked her. When she was young, her father had not done his daily prayers. She did not know that he had started. She had been separated from her father for so long. It had been difficult to stay in touch during her years in England without papers. After that, it seemed that too much had happened. She no longer needed a father. She reflected that she was an orphan now. Her mother's heart failure twelve years ago had also been a shock. She thought her mother was indestructible. It was her father whom she always thought was vulnerable to the things the world threw at him. She wanted to go to the funeral with her daughter. She had spoken to her husband, who had given his permission. They were in line. She was used to the derisive looks.

She and her twelve-year-old daughter wore black niqabs that entirely covered their bodies but for the narrow slit for their eyes. She wore long black gloves- the type that some women wore with stylish gowns to the opera- which covered her arms up to the elbows. Her daughter wore those gloves too. Azeeza had lived in London for twenty years. She started wearing the niqab in her second year. A year before she met her husband. She had never been able to use her University of Maiduguri law degree. Her husband drove a cab. He had dropped them off at the airport before his shift began.

When, as she expected, the man behind the counter asked her and her daughter to go into a separate room where they would have to disrobe in front of female security officers, she clutched her boarding pass and muttered under her breath in Arabic "Why won't you leave us alone? We are Muslims and believe in the One God."

The moon had been swallowed by large clouds and the night had darkened when the Peugeot's lights cut past the gate of the Lake Chad Club and turned onto the Gombole road which lead to their home. The headlights caught the dust that lingered in the night air, rising from the black tarmac like levitating particles. Professor Kyari looked out of the windshield at the empty road. He turned his head often to check on his children. Halima was sleeping with her head in her sister's lap. Azeeza's eyes were closed but she was awake. She was thinking of Abbai and the kiss. She let her mind slide into an indulgent daydream in which she and Abbai were married adults driving away from the Lake Chad Club to go to their home together. Azeeza smiled. She was happy.

Ismailia looked out of the window, his eyes open. There were very few cars. On the side of the road, a few men were gathered around a kerosene fire, smoking cigarettes. He could hear them laughing. Lateef had apologised for making fun of his mother. He had sworn never to do it again. Ismailia had not understood the way Lateef fought. He still felt confused about what had happened between them, but he was full and excited and looked forward to another weekend at the club.

Mrs. Kyari was looking out the windshield. She coyly turned to make a short glance at her husband. She could see he noticed because of the small smile that lingered in the corner of his mouth. They were happy.